I0779217

TULA
And the Choctaw Trail of Tears

G.K. Montilla

TULA
And the Choctaw Trail of Tears

G.K. Montilla

ISBN: 978-1-965943-03-8

Table of Contents

Dedication

This book is dedicated to the families of the Choctaw people who endured the unthinkable hardships during the Trail of Tears. May your courage and resilience in the face of overwhelming suffering never be forgotten, and may the memory of your loved ones, who were lost to the cruelty of forced removal, live on in every word written here.

To those whose lives were forever altered by the events before and after the 1830's, we honor your legacy. May this work serve as a testament to your strength, a reminder of the profound injustices inflicted upon your people, and a call to remember the enduring spirit of those who survived and those who perished. Your stories, your sacrifices, and your memories will remain an indelible part of our shared history.

Introduction

The Treaty of Dancing Rabbit Creek, signed on September 27, 1830, marked a significant and tragic turning point in the history of the Choctaw Nation and Native Americans as a whole. As the first treaty negotiated after the passage of the Indian Removal Act of 1830, it set the stage for widespread displacement.

Under the treaty, the Choctaw Nation ceded approximately 11 million acres of ancestral land in present-day Mississippi to the U.S. government. In return, they were promised land in Indian Territory, now Oklahoma, where they could supposedly live without interference. However, the majority of the Choctaw people were pressured or forced to relocate, enduring the arduous journey known as the Trail of Tears. Thousands of Choctaw died from hunger, disease, and exposure during the migration.

While the treaty technically allowed some Choctaw to remain in Mississippi as U.S. citizens, those who stayed faced severe discrimination and were often coerced and manipulated into giving up their remaining land. Promises made by the U.S. government in the treaty, such as provisions, transportation, and protection during relocation, were largely unfulfilled, adding to the hardships faced by the Choctaw people. The forced removal severed them from their ancestral lands, sacred sites, and cultural heritage, compelling them to rebuild their communities under harsh conditions in Indian Territory.

This treaty had broader implications for Native Americans, as it set a precedent for similar removal treaties and the enforcement of the Indian Removal Act. Many Indigenous peoples experienced immense suffering and loss of life as a result, and the long-term consequences included the erosion of Native American cultures, languages, and traditions.

Despite these hardships, the Choctaw Nation survived and continues to uphold their heritage and sovereignty in Oklahoma and beyond, serving as a testament to their resilience in the face of injustice.

Chapter 1: The Savagery

Beautiful rays of sunlight fall through the tall Cypress trees and onto the slow-moving Mississippi river below. Choirs of finches, cardinals, and doves sing as they fly from one branch to another. A gentle breeze sways the tall river grasses on the riverbanks. Ducks slowly glide downstream, then paddle back to their previous position. Large cumulus clouds crown a riverside clearing adorned by wildflowers.

Here, a Choctaw tribe has settled by the waterside. Children play and run to and fro in the camp as adults busy themselves in their morning tasks. Some prepare food or tend to their fire. Some tend to animal pelts; others are feeding the horses. But everyone seems to be preparing for something. An old grandma, holding a small pair of pants, chases a naked little boy out of a shelter—she can hardly keep up.

They boy runs straight to the trees and jumps into a tall hydrangea bush to make his escape. The little boy crouches inside the bush but does not know his behind is hanging out and is completely visible. Grandma can't help but break out in laughter.

Sparrow, a young mother breastfeeding her newborn baby by a large open fire, laughs as she sees the little boy hiding from his grandma. Sparrow's braids are adorned with flowers; her necklaces and beads hang from her neck down to her breasts, the beads jingling as she laughs. She looks down at her own baby boy suckling on her nipple and smiles even brighter. She adores him, and it shows in her eyes as she leans forward and kisses him on the head.

She sits on a large, broken log and nods her head at her baby as she admires him. She closes her eyes for a moment and takes a deep breath. The smell of burning wood, flowers, and earth soothe her mind. She slowly opens her eyes and grins at her two daughters that now stand opposite her, on the other side of the fire. Pride builds up inside her heart as she sees them smiling back at her.

Isi, the oldest daughter, is fifteen. She's a beautiful girl with dark caramel skin and long, jet-black hair down to her waist. She's tall for her age and has outgrown her clothing. Her pant bottoms reach up to her shins, and the sleeves of her shirt are halfway up her forearms. Tula, her younger sister with a slightly lighter complexion, stands beside her. Even though Tula is only ten, she is stocky and strong. A tomboy, she likes to run around with no shirt on. Her hands and feet covered in mud.

"There they are. My beautiful girls!" Sparrow says with a smile. "Tula where is your top?"

Tula pats her chest, covering it with mud, then puts her hands on her waist and says, "If the boys can play like this, then so can I!"

"Why are your hands and feet covered in mud?" Sparrow asks.

"I was playing with the frogs," Tula answers.

Sparrow looks at Isi, who shakes her head at her sister. "Isi, take your sister downriver and make sure she cleans up. You should bathe yourself as well. Take the clothes I made for you, please. Those are too small."

Isi looks down at her clothing. "Father gave me these. I remember him better when I'm wearing them."

"I understand, but if you continue to wear them, they will rip…" Sparrow says. She points to a large stone by the river. "On the large boulder over there, the clothes I made. I put them there for you. Take them."

"I will mother," Isi replies.

"Girls…be careful, be watchful, and be mindful of your surroundings." Sparrow looks at Isi, pulling her toward her with a powerful gaze. "When I'm not present, she is your responsibility. If there is any trouble—any whatsoever—bring your sister and yourself right back to me." After receiving a nod from her older daughter, Sparrow looks at young Tula. "Listen to your sister and obey. You also have to look out for her and make sure she is all right."

"I will mama," says Tula.

Sparrow smiles. She looks at both of her girls with tenderness and no small sense of pride.

"I love you more than you will ever know. We have a long journey ahead, so please hurry back. Go now. I'll see you soon."

As soon as she finishes speaking the fire in front of Sparrow suddenly flares up, as a burning log within falls once it can bear its weight no more. Everyone is startled, but that fright quickly gives way to laughter as the girls take their leave.

Isi and Tula turn around and walk toward the river, holding hands as they leave their mother. They make their way toward the rock Sparrow pointed to and Isi grabs the clothing made for her. Isi holds them up to her chest and looks back at her mother, sharing one more smile before Isi leads her sister into the forest.

Sparrow trails the girls with her eyes, following every movement her daughters make. She looks down to check on the baby at her breast and begins to rock back and forth. When she looks up again to get a glimpse of the girls, they are no longer to be seen. The mother looks around into the camp and sees people walking to and fro, then she looks back into the direction of where her girls went. A look of deep concern crosses her face.

The girls make their way through the bushes and the thick forest vegetation until they arrive in a smaller clearing a little further downriver. The place is secluded, opening to the river's edge, and it is covered with many types of native flowers and wildlife. Rabbits and birds scurry into the forest as the girls enter the clearing. Tula runs right up to the river's edge, quickly removes what's left of her clothes, and jumps into the water. Isi begins to take her clothes off and looks at Tula moving around in the water and laughs at her.

"What are you doing?" Isi asks.

"Look. I'm a duck!" says Tula as she purses her lips and flaps her arms.

Isi finishes taking off her clothes and slowly enters the water, looking around carefully. She shivers as the water hits her tummy, and softly begins to pour water on her shoulders and arms. "Tula stop playing around and start cleaning yourself," says Isi.

But Tula does not listen and instead continues to swim around. Tula looks over to the other bank of the river and sees a deer within the tall grasses that sway with the breeze. She looks up to the sky as she floats and catches the rays of sunlight piercing through the large cumulus clouds.

"Why do we have to leave? I love it here," says Tula as she lets the current slowly carry her away from Isi.

Isi dunks her head into the water and begins to lather her armpits with leaves. She looks over at Tula, still playing around, and holds the leaves out to her.

"I told you already: everyone is going north to a new land. We don't have a choice. Now come over here and let me clean you up!" answers Isi, but Tula continues to drift downriver. "Don't go too far!" Isi shouts.

Suddenly Isi stops bathing. She senses something is wrong. She looks around and quickly submerges herself into the water. Slowly, she comes up out of the water to her neck and looks over to Tula, who is now further down river playing.

"Tula. Tula, get over here!" Isi says, but her voice is drowned out by the sound of the water, and Tula cannot hear her.

*   *   *

Back at the camp, the morning carries on like usual. At the edge of the camp two men talk as they pet and feed their horses. Suddenly, a small naked boy runs out of the forest, and into the camp, a dog running right beside him. The men, startled, look at the boy running past them and immediately look back at the forest where the boy emerged. Both men put their hands on the knives at their hips, expecting whatever frightened the boy to come out as well. The little boy continues to run through the whole camp, past the women and men working, as well as the other little kids that are playing. He runs all the way to the other end of the camp where Sparrow is still sitting by the fire, nursing her child.

BANG!

The sound of a loud gunshot goes off and startles the camp. Screams ring out next, and panic ensues. A few men quickly grab their rifles as they look around, not knowing where the sound came from.

But Sparrow's baby, still at her breast, is slowly coated with blood. The young, running boy abruptly stops and turns around. He sees Sparrow looking at him with glazed-over eyes. Her mouth is wide open, and saliva streams down her chin. There is a large wound in her head and blood drips from there onto the crying baby weakly clutched in her hands. Sparrow leans forward, and more blood pours onto the baby's face, and into his mouth, causing him to gargle.

The young boy looks past Sparrow, to the edge of the forest at the other end of the camp. Suddenly a tall and broad pale-white soldier emerges from behind the tree line. The blue-eyed, red-haired grizzly of a man is dressed in a sloppy U.S. Army uniform. He smiles, his rifle still smoking as he carries it past the trees. His eyes glisten with excitement. He can see the fear and panic in the camp. His smile only subsides momentarily when spits his tobacco on the ground.

"Bullseye! Hot damn that was a good shot!" says Captain Francis.

The naked little boy sees the captain and runs to Sparrow's lap, but she does not respond. The boy looks at the tree line again, and sese U.S. soldiers rush into the camp, shooting the native men standing by the horses. The little boy shakes Sparrow, but she has left the world behind. Her head leans forward a little bit further, causing more blood and brains to fall onto her baby, now drowning beneath her.

Chaos breaks out in the camp as women and children run. A few native men rush the soldiers, but are gunned down immediately. More soldiers emerge from the forest, flooding the camp with terror.

Captain Francis reloads his rifle, a gleeful, wicked smile upon his face as he sees the village now overwhelmed by soldiers on horseback. They ride past him and into the camp, killing indiscriminately—every native they see.

A native man throws an axe at a soldier, striking him in the face, the first sign that it will not be a bloodless victory for the soldiers. As the man goes to retrieve his axe, another shot rings out, and he feels a sudden sting in his chest. His death comes swiftly, and he falls face-first on the soldier he killed.

A group of soldiers find women sheltering their young inside of a tent, but they are offered no reprieve. The soldiers line them up outside, and has them face a firing squad, with no hope for mercy. Behind them, an old native man rushes the soldiers with a large knife, but he cannot reach him. He is trampled by a soldier on a horse.

On the edge of the camp, a young native woman watches as a native man catches a bayonet stab to the chest. She sees the man fall, and she herself drops to the ground. She comes out of the bushes slowly, and crawls to the fallen man. She grabs the rifle from the native and quickly runs back to climb a tree. She positions herself between two large branches, tears flowing from her face as she looks down on the horrific scene below.

Her people are being slaughtered.

She aims her rifle at a soldier aiming at a young boy and shoots him in the chest. She turns to her right and shoots another soldier on horseback in the head. The man falls sideways out of the saddle, but his foot catches in the stirrup, and he is dragged by his horse into the woods. As she positions herself to shoot someone else, return fire hits the tree, and a bullet grazes her leg. She reflexively reaches for the wound, and is shot again on the shoulder. She falls from the tree, unable to properly brace herself before she collides to the ground.

A young soldier with a smoking rifle runs up to her, and grabs her by her hair, he punches her in the eye, and she falls backward. The soldier then takes the butt of his rifle and hits her in the nose. Blood gushes out of the woman's face like a river. He looks around and sees that no one is paying attention to him. He grabs the girl by the throat, picks her up and slams her up against the tree she was firing from. The soldier takes his knife and begins to cut off her clothing. The woman's dress falls to the ground.

"What do you think you are doing soldier!? Captain Francis yells.

The soldier turns around and sees the captain looking straight at him, and he freezes in fear.

"You a dog fucker, O'Riley"? the captain asks. Before the soldier can answer, the captain pistol whips the young woman against the side of her head, the blow knocking her out. "No fucking 'til the killings done," he screams. "Now get out there and make something of yourself soldier. Move it!"

The soldier runs out of the woods and into the camp with his rifle. The captain looks down at the unconscious young woman, glancing at her for just a moment longer. He turns around and follows the soldier back into the chaotic scene. The captain walks past soldiers killing natives, and natives fighting back. A native young man runs up to the captain with a knife and tries to stab him in the chest. The captain drops his rifle and grabs the native's knife hand before it can come close to its target. The captain is much stronger, and he easily overpowers the boy. He grabs the boy by the throat, turns the teen's hand around, and pushes the knife into his eye socket slowly. The boy begins to scream, and the captain smiles as he watches the knife enter deeper into the skull, all while life exits the boy's body. The boy finally goes completely limp, and the captain pulls the knife out.

"Not today…" says the captain. As he throws the lifeless body down on the ground like a rag doll, he spits on it. The captain looks up and continues to walk through the camp, casually shooting natives as he walks to the other side of the camp. The captain finally reaches Sparrow's body, still sitting in front of the fire. The young native boy that ran out of the woods and through the camp is still standing there, frozen in shock, looking at Captain Francis.

The captain stands over Sparrow's shoulder and looks down. Her baby is covered in blood but still breathing, barely. Captain Francis studies the hole in Sparrow's head. He puts his finger in it and looks in, then he looks over at the boy and says, "Pretty good shot, no?"

The boy does not answer, but tears begin to fall from his bloodshot eyes. The captain becomes upset. He kicks Sparrow's body into the fire face-first, baby and all. Blood-curdling cries come from underneath the burning body as the baby burns alive. The captain spits tobacco on

Sparrow's body, then picks up his rifle and points it at the boy's head.

Isi suddenly appears from the bushes, half-clothed, and jumps in between the captain and the boy. She quickly grabs the boy, kneels and lifts her hand, pleading.

"Please. Please, don't. Please," Isi cries as she holds the child.

*　　　*　　　*

In the meantime, Tula continues to drift downriver, as she looks at the beautiful flowers on the banks of the Mississippi. She closes her eyes, and smiles as the sunrays touch her face when they pierce the clouds above. Suddenly, Tula hears someone whistle. She lifts her head and looks back to where Isi was standing just a minute ago.

She's gone.

She hears the whistle again and looks around until she finally sees one of the tribe elders on the other side of the river hiding amongst tall grasses. He looks terrified, and motions for her to come to him.

"What's the matter?" Tula asks.

The old man points toward the camp, Tula turns and looks. Her mouth drops as she sees plumes of smoke rising from the trees where the tribe's camp is located. She looks back to the old man, and he puts his finger over his lips, signaling her to not make a sound, then the man motions for her to come to him. Tula swims to him, emerging from water, but with her eyes fixated on the smoke. It grows darker, and bigger, with every passing moment. The old man takes his mantle off his shoulders and covers naked Tula. She reaches out and hugs him.

"What's happening, Nashoba?" Tula asks.

"Trouble," he replies. "We need to stay out of sight."

Nashoba picks Tula up and quickly carries her into the forest, away from the riverbank.

*   *   *

Back at the camp, Captain Francis has put his rifle down. He slowly moves the tobacco in his mouth as he stares at Isi. She shelters the young boy in her arms and weeps. A young soldier runs up to Captain Francis from behind.

"Captain. Captain!" the young soldier shouts as he approaches.

The captain slowly turns to look at the young man. The soldier stops short, right in front of the captain, salutes and tries to catch his breath. The soldier's face and uniform are covered in blood, his right sleeve slightly ripped off at the shoulder and fresh scratch marks are visible on his neck.

The captain salutes the boy, frustrated that he's being interrupted. "What's the matter son?"

"We've captured additional men in the forest. It looks like they were coming back from a hunt. They had a lot of game with them," The soldier says.

"Blessing in disguise. We'll need food for the way back," replies the captain, as he turns around and looks into the camp, and the gory spectacle before him. Bleeding women and men cry as they are beaten and killed by soldiers. Children are dragged from the dead bodies of their mothers and tied up like cattle. Dead bodies are everywhere, and the shelters are on fire, with not much left to salvage. The captain takes a deep breath and speaks to the young soldier beside him. "Let's wrap this up Sergeant. Round up these godless animals and get them ready to move."

"Yes sir!" shouts the soldier, and then he quickly walks back into the camp shouting. "Alright men! Grab whatever is still alive, tie them up in groups, and let's get ready to move! Let go! Let's go!"

The captain turns around, his attention back on Isi and the boy. Isi squirms in fear when he turns around. He walks around the large fire and grabs Isi by the arm, roughly pulling her up to him as she holds the child. As he walks her around the fire, Isi sees her mother's body burning and lets the boy go.

Isi screams in shock, horror and despair, reaching out with her arms to her mother's burning body as she is dragged away by the uncaring captain. Her cries fill the camp, resonating above everything else. The captain hits her in the head with the end of his rifle and knocks her out, her body going completely limp as she is dragged like a rag doll. The little boy follows them, not knowing where else to go.

*   *   *

Tula and Nashoba watch the camp from the other side of the river, crouched, hiding in the very tall grasses by the riverbank. Tula weeps, she looks at the old man and tries to stand up, but the old man hugs her and puts his hand over her mouth.

"If they hear us, we're dead" he whispers softly.

"We have to help them," she whispers back.

"If you go, you will only share in their misery," he replied.

Tula nods in agreement.

They watch as the captain drags Isi's body and threw her at the feet of a group of women that were being tied up. Soldiers scavenge the dead bodies for trinkets and souvenirs, and some scalp the dead. The cries of weeping women and children fill the air. Men and women are picked up and dragged away from their dead children's bodies. They are gathered up into groups and tied up like cattle at gunpoint. The captain oversees the whole operation as he puts a cigarette together. He sees private O'Riley coming out of the woods with the girl the captain knocked out earlier, now naked and bleeding. The captain motions for him to bring her to the rest of the group. The sergeant comes up to the captain and says,

"We'll be ready to go in two minutes sir."

"Thank you, Sergeant, it looks like we're pretty much done here."

A soldier brings a beautiful black horse to the captain, the red-haired brute patting the animal in appreciation. He nods at the soldier, mounts the horse and lights his cigarette. He looks at the bound natives, and at the soldiers lined up and ready to march. The ones on horseback have surrounded the group, and look to the captain.

"All right, move out!" yells the captain.

What's left of the tribe is slowly herded away from the camp like sheep into the forest.

*   *   *

The sun begins to hang low in the western sky. A few hours have past. Tula and Nashoba slowly enter the camp, tears flowing from their eyes. They move slowly, completely taken back by the scene before them. There are dead bodies everywhere—men, women and children alike. Some have missing limbs; some are half dressed; they all have multiple bullet wounds and are covered in blood. Their faces express the pain they felt as they died.

"So much death..." Tula whispers, then continues louder. "There's blood everywhere, rivers of it."

"All the white man ever brings is death…"

Tula then sees the remains of her mother's body in the middle of the smoke and ashes a few yards away. She runs and cries out in pain. "No, Mama!"

Tula reaches the body and tries to pull it out of the ashes, but it's too heavy for her. Nashoba runs over and helps her. They place the body face up. The whole upper body is burned beyond recognition, the baby fused to Sparrow's chest, both withered husks of what they once were.

Tula falls on her knees. She tilts her head back and opens her mouth wide to cry, but no sound comes out. She is devastated. Needing to tear her emotions from her chest, Tula takes a deep breath in, and then lets out a fierce and blood-curdling cry,

Nashoba kneels beside her and weeps. Tula's haunting cries fill the camp and resonate through the forest, willing birds to take flight. The old man puts his arm around Tula and tries to console her.

"These savages, I don't understand it," Nashoba says. "We cannot stay here, it's not safe."

Tula tries to wipe her eyes, but tears continue to flow. "But we can't leave our people trike this!"

"We don't know if the soldiers will return. If we stay here, we die," replied Nashoba.

Tula takes a long deep look into Nashoba's eyes, then she looks at her mother's body. She slowly leans forward and kisses what's left of her head.

"What do we do?" asks Tula.

"We run. We need to get far from this place. There is only death here," says the old man.

Tula looks at Nashoba, then looks up at the sky. As tears continue to fall down her face, in a trembling voice she voices another concern. "I have not seen my sister Isi amongst the dead. That means she still lives… She's all I have left."

Nashoba stands and takes a good long look around what remains of their camp. He then turns his attention to the tracks on the ground. They lead in the direction that the soldiers exited the camp and entered the forest. The old man turns around, looks at Tula, and takes a deep breath.

"We can follow their trail and see where they go. We check to see if your sister is with them, but we keep our distance," says the old man.

The old man walks toward the edge of the forest and waits for Tula. She quickly gets up and stands beside the old man and puts her hand on his arm. Nashoba begins to look around. He takes a few steps into the forest and kneels. There are tracks everywhere, but they all lead in one direction.

"The tracks lead east, deep into the forest. Remember, when we catch up, we keep our distance," Nashoba says.

Tula nods in agreement. The old man puts his hand on her cheek and caresses it sweetly, then he runs into the forest. Tula follows right behind.

Meanwhile, the caravan of soldiers and natives slowly move through a large clearing. They just exit the forest, with the tall trees behind them swaying in the wind. The area is comprised of tall grasses, bushes and just a few trees here and there. The open sky above them starts to turn gray. All the natives have their hands bound, forced to walk behind the cavalry horses they're tied to. The soldiers who steadily laugh and jest as they move are not paying close attention to them, involved in their own conversations. A small child at the end of the line stumbles and falls from fatigue. The toddler scratches his knees badly and the wounds begin to bleed. A young native man quickly moves to try to help the young child, but a soldier on horseback quickly rides up and prevents him by kicking him away. The soldier smiles as the boy struggles to get up several times and keeps falling. The force of the rope around his hands being pulled by the horses makes it difficult for him. The boy falls repeatedly, over and over, until his head hits a rock on the ground, and he falls unconscious, his little body dragged belly-down by the horse in front.

A woman sees the child and looks at the soldier. His yellow tobacco smile glistens in the sun as he leans back and laughs.

The young native man sees her getting ready to do something and says, "Nita, don't… They will kill you."

But Nita does not listen. She sees the soldier is distracted and hurries to help the young boy. She picks up the child, now with long, deep, bloody scratches on his face and body, and cradles him in her arms. She begins to pull twigs and leaves stuck to his flesh. As she brushes dirt off the child's forehead, she looks up to see where the soldier is. Her face is met with the heel of the soldier's boot. The woman drops the child, and falls to the ground, her forehead split open, her blood pouring onto the ground. She quickly gets up in defiance, wipes her bloody face and looks over at the young boy being dragged on his back now. The soldier looks at her with fiery hatred, rides up to her side, pulls out his pistol and points it at her. Nita stares at him in defiance.

"You try that again, dog…" the soldier says, motioning to the boy being dragged with his gun. "Go ahead, go get him, bitch."

Captain Francis, riding in the middle of the caravan had been observing the whole exchange. He looks at the boy being dragged unconscious, and the bloodied woman looking at the soldier. He looks up at the sky and sees how the weather is quickly changing. Clouds cover the gray sky, and it grows darker far quicker than he would like.

"Company halt!" yells the captain, and everyone suddenly stops. "Sergeant Daniels!" yells the captain, and the sergeant rides up to his side and salutes.

"Sir," answers Sergeant Daniels.

"We set up camp right here. Get Mr. Johnson to get a fire going and make supper with the game these Indians caught," says the captain.

"Yes sir!" says the Sargent, and he rides away barking orders. "You heard him men, we set up camp here! Get the tents up. Move it, move it!"

The soldier on horseback that was intimidating the bloodied woman puts his pistol away and follows the sergeant. The bloodied native woman stumbles over to the boy on the ground, who's still unconscious. She picks him up and holds him close to her chest. Blood from her forehead drips onto the boy. She tries to wipe it off with her forearm, but it makes it worse. She begins to cry. She looks around and sees the captain already looking at her stoically. He quickly looks away.

The captain gets off his horse, he looks at a group of soldiers, and then points to the natives. "You men, round up the savages, and set up a perimeter to guard them. No one escapes!"

The men quickly move to action, some undoing the knots that tie the natives to the horses. Others push and shove them into a tighter group.

*   *   *

Half a mile away, on top of a hill, Tula and Nashoba lay on their bellies, behind a grassy overgrowth. They watch the soldiers as they set up camp. They lay still as the minutes turn to hours, and a military camp appears before them. Fires are lit, tents erected, and the noises in the camp seem to grow louder as the night falls.

Nashoba taps Tula on the shoulder, and points to the east. "There'd a white man's camp, about a half day's distance away from here. I suspect that's where they are going," says the old man.

Tula nods and look back down at the camp. A full moon shines down on the clearing below, with just a few clouds lit up by the moonlight. The sound of crickets, frogs and other critters of the night encompass the area.

*　　　*　　　*

Meanwhile, inside the camp, some soldiers eat and drink as they tell stories and laugh around the campfires. Some of them are already sleeping in their tents, as guards patrol the perimeter of the camp.

Captain Francis sits on a small rock by one of the fires, a flask of alcohol in one hand, and a cigarette in the other. He looks past his men. With glazed over eyes he looks in the direction of the native captives at the other end of the camp. The natives have gathered in a large group. Without fire, and without food, they are exhausted from the trip. Many are still bloodied and bruised from the horrors of the day.

The captain climbs to his feet. Some of the soldiers take note and watch him as he makes his way to the natives. The soldiers tap each other to get everyone's attention as to what the captain is about to do. Isi, who is holding a sleeping little girl in her arms watches as the captain approaches. He takes one long last puff of his cigarette and throws it on the ground. He walks right up to Isi and the little girl, takes a deep pull from his flask and wipes his mouth before he puts it away in his vest pocket. The captain takes a good look at Isi, and then the rest of the natives sitting on the ground. He becomes disgusted by the sight of them. He opens his trousers and begins to urinate on Isi and the little girls. Isi gets angry, and adjusts her feet to get up, but soldiers guarding them quickly point their rifles at Isi. She stays seated as the captain finishes off.

The captain turns to one of the soldiers holding a rifle then. "Have someone gather up the scraps and whatever food's left in the pot, and give it to these dogs, soldier."

"Will do, sir," answers the soldier.

Nita, the woman who was earlier punished for picking up the young boy, sits amid the group. The captain's eyes fall on her as she looks at him with vehement hatred. The woman slowly rises, the wound on her head continuing to ooze blood. Her dress is stained crimson. She wipes her face, as the captain folds his arms expecting something to happen. One of the elders in the tribe tries to get her to sit back down by pulling on her dress, but she slaps her hand away.

Nita holds up her bloodied hands and dares to speak to the man. "You…you've killed our fathers, our mothers, our sisters and our brothers. You've killed my husband, my children, and taken all hope. You've taken our land, and if we had anything else, you would've taken that too."

The captain smiles and shakes his head as he takes chewing tobacco and packs it inside his lower lip.

The guards pay close attention as Nita continues.

"I curse you; I curse you all…I curse your children, and your children's children. This land…my people's land—that you have stolen from us—it will be a curse to you and your offspring, and you will find no peace in it!" Nita then points her bloody index finger at Captain Francis. When she does, a drop of her blood hits his forehead. "And you! You think you are a predator. But I call on the spirits of vengeance today to avenge me and my people of your wrath! To seek you, and hunt you until you are consumed, until your memory is taken from existence. You are now the prey! You are the hunted! Die! *Die!*"

One of the guards strikes Nita in the head with his fist, and as she falls, he knees her in the nose. Nita falls to the ground unconscious, face-first into the dirt. A native man quickly grabs Nita and pulls her to his lap and tries to wipe the blood off her face.

Captain Francis wipes his forehead, walks up to the soldier that struck Nita down, and pats him on the back.

"Did you understand a word she said? What the fuck was that all about?" asked the captain.

"I don't know sir. I don't speak dog," replied the soldier. The soldiers and the captain laugh for a few seconds, until it becomes a bit awkward.

The captain walks away. He checks his pocket watch, and winds it a few times, when suddenly, he screams loudly and falls to the ground. He is quickly surrounded by his men. As he tries to pull his right boot off, one of the soldiers helps him, then falls on his butt. A small black snake jumps out of the boot and slithers away. The captain quickly takes his side arm out and shoots it before it can enter the tall brush.

One of the soldiers goes and looks for the snake. The captain looks at his foot. He has a small snake bite on his ankle, and almost at once, his foot begins to turn red.

The soldier returns with the dead snake, a look of relief in his eyes. "You'll be ok, Captain; this one is not poisonous."

The captain is helped up by his soldiers, but once on his feet, he pushes them away from him and looks at Nita, still laying on the man's lap, unconscious. He looks down at his ankle. It's swollen from the bite, and slightly bleeding. He then looks back at the woman and spits tobacco on the ground.

"Let me take care of the wound sir," one of the soldiers says.

The captain nods in agreement. He holds the soldier's shoulder as he slowly makes his way to his tent.

*   *   *

The night passes slowly. The moon and stars fade away. Daylight brings with it a cloudy morning. Mist and drizzling rain dampen the ground, and the hearts of the people in the group. Birds chirp, and horses neigh as the soldiers pack up, and carry on casual conversation. The captain is fully dressed and sits on his horse as he observes his men work.

Surrounded by soldiers, the native men and women stand in a tight group. Isi is among them, holding the hand of the boy she saved back at her camp. The fires are extinguished as the drizzle turns into hard rain, quickly transforming the ground to mud. Just a few feet away from the group, Nita's body lies in that mud, her face distorted from the pain, her eyes and mouth still open. One of the soldiers walks up to Nita's body and inspects it. He rips her beaded necklace off, and pockets it. He turns round and sees Isi staring at him in complete dismay of what he's doing. When Isi sees that he's looking at her, she quickly puts her head down and shields her face. The soldier stares at her for a moment then walks away. As he does, he realizes that the captain had been watching the whole exchange.

The captain holds out his hand to the soldier. "I'd like to keep that one son, if you don't mind"

The soldier places the beaded necklace in the captain's hand and says.

"Of course, sir."

The captain looks over at Isi stoically, as she watches him take the necklace and put it in his coat pocket.

The rain picking up sees that the camp is completely broken down, and everyone seems to be ready to move. The captain looks over at the sergeant, who give him a strong positive nod. The captain lifts his right hand and points east.

"Onward…March!" shouts the captain.

A group moves, forming a distinct line as they choose their route. Toward the end of the line, horses are pulling the ropes the natives are tied to. The men and women struggle to walk in the rain, and through the thick and heavy mud. The soldiers bringing up the rear jeer and jest as they watch the struggle.

*   *   *

Tula and Nashoba watch as they slowly make their way out of the valley, until they completely disappear from view. They are wet, but unfazed by the rain. They quickly make their way down the hill to where the soldiers stayed. Nashoba slowly emerges from the brush and stands very still as he looks around. No one remains. He whistles to signal Tula and walks toward Nita's body. Tula comes out of the bushes and slowly walks toward the old man, carefully looking in all directions.

They stand for a few minutes in the heavy downpour, looking down at Nita's body without saying a word. Nita's eyes are pointed up so much so that almost only the whites of her eyes are showing. Her mouth is open, filled with water, as if she was still about to say something. Lighting flashes in the distance, quickly followed by roaring thunder. The wind suddenly picks up and hits them from the east. Tula and Nashoba lift their heads, look at each other, and begin to walk in that direction.

*   *   *

About a mile east from Tula and the old man, the rain comes down in sheets. The trees and the brush are bright green from the rain. A solitary bird chirps underneath a tree branch, but the sound of the rain is overpowering. A single frog in the mud is stepped on by the hoof of a horse, the hoof descends a few inches and when it lifts, the frog jumps out of the hole. Horse after horse pass it, until the hands of a young native boy reach down and pick it up.

The group of soldiers escorting the natives approach a U.S. Army fortified outpost. On a very muddy trail leading up to its front gates the group comes to a stop. Lightning strikes in the distance, and thunder rolls as the sound of the rain hitting the muddy puddles seems to grow louder. The wooden walls of the fort look like they have seen their share of battle, partially burnt and rebuilt in several places.

The guard on top of the tower facing the gate yells down to someone below. "Open the gate! They're back… Open the gate!"

The large wooden gates slowly swing open, and soldiers come out to greet the incoming party. With intrigue, they call other soldiers to come and look at the natives, and quickly more soldiers come out and gawk at the sight of the tied-up prisoners as they pass by and enter the fort. But not everyone is amused, as a few soldiers that stand around a campfire underneath a shelter simply watch from a distance, then continue their conversation.

Captain Francis rides up to one of the soldiers watching them enter. "Tell Major O'Connell I've arrived."

"Yes sir!" replies the soldier, who quickly runs into the fort toward some cabins.

The captain looks over to a group of soldiers standing by the gate. "You men: take these Indians and lock them up tight!"

"Yes sir!" they reply, and quickly run to the horses that they are tied up to, take the ropes, and pull the people into the fort by force.

"Good job men," the captain says. "Get some food and take some rest. You've earned it. You are relieved!"

All his men begin to disperse into the encampment, laughing, and talking about the previous day's massacre to the troops welcoming them in.

Within the fort stables, a soldier with a pitchfork moves hay around from a large pile in the corner to the horse stalls. Another soldier removes a saddle from a horse, while another polishes a saddle on a large table positioned against a wall. The stables are large, and dimly lit with gas lamps on the walls. The rain is finally letting up, but it is still loud as it hits against the roof off the stables. The wind, however, seems to be picking up. A shutter on one of the windows keeps slamming violently against the outside wall.

The large stables door open, and Captain Francis walks in. The soldiers stand at attention and salute.

"At ease men. I just came to bring you my horse," says the captain.

The soldiers continue to work.

The young soldier polishing the saddle on a large table comes up to the captain and takes the reins from him. The captain takes note of the good looking blond-haired, blue-eyed boy and watches him as he begins to take the saddle off his horse.

"What's your name soldier? I've never seen you before," says the captain.

"Name's Edward, sir," the lad replied.

The captain was about to say something, but the sudden appearance of a soldier running into the stables distracted him. His hair stands straight up from the wind. Everyone turns around to see him.

The soldier stands in front of the captain and salutes. "Captain Francis, Major O'Connell requests your presence immediately!"

"Where is he?" asks the captain.

Outside, all the natives are being ushered from the open jail into some of the cabins that stand against the fort walls. The captain points to them, a query upon his lips. "What is this?"

The soldier turns around and sees that the captain is pointing to the natives. "Oh, yeah that's Major O'Connell's orders, sir," replies the soldier.

The captain is infuriated. He quickly walks out of the stables and makes his way to the major's cabin. Soldiers salute as he passes but he ignores them. A strong wind almost knocks him over as he walks up a flooded pebble pathway leading to the major's cabin. The captain knocks on the door, but there is no answer. He slowly enters the cabin.

Wooden walls decorated with a few hanging pictures are lit up by the fireplace made of stone on the side wall. A small desk opposite the door has papers and envelopes falling off of it. A gas lamp on the desk lights that corner of the room. Captain Francis stands beside the door and tries to compose himself. Major O'Connell, a man from New York with a presence to match enters the room. The Major grabs his spectacles from his desk and sits where they had just been. He shuffles through some papers until he finds one in particular that he is looking for. The major tweaks his mustache and speaks to his fellow officer. "Says here, Captain, that the tribe you went to fetch is made up of over two hundred men and women." The major stands, throws his spectacles back on the desk and looks at the captain with disdain. "How many Indians did you bring back with you, Captain?" asks the major.

The captain hesitates to answer, but the major raises his eyebrows and intimidates the captain to answer.

"Well…around seventy-three, sir. No, strike that. There are seventy-two. One died during travel. Sir."

The major looks down at the report in his hand and drops it on his desk. He comes out from behind his desk and stands right in front of the captain. The captain stands a foot taller than the major. The height difference is very evident as the major looks up to him to make eye contact.

"That report is only two weeks old captain, where are my remaining one hundred and thirty Indians?"

The captain looks straight head and does not make eye contact with the major. "Sir, we arrived at their camp yesterday morning and were immediately met with force. We were attacked…"

The major interrupts him, and angrily prods the captain's chest with his index finger. "You attacked their camp sir; you killed them indiscriminately and brought what was left of them into my camp, tied up like animals!" yells the major.

"Sir, we didn't… We—" the captain begins to speak.

The major interrupts him, his voice growing ever louder. "What were your orders Captain?"

The captain, angry and red-faced, begins to breath heavily, his lower jaw protruding outward.

"What were your goddamned orders, Captain?" The major shouts, spitting now on the captain's face.

"Find the tribe settled by the river, and escort them to the departure point so that they can join the caravans traveling north. Sir," replies Captain Francis.

The major turns around and walks over to his desk. "Escort them… Escort them, Captain. That's exactly what your orders said. We're here to keep the peace now, we are no longer at war with these people. We won, damn it!"

"Sir, we've—" the captain begins to say something.

"Shut up" barks the major. He walks behind his desk and sits down. He looks at the captain in disgust and shakes his head. "There was a time when events like this went unchecked, Captain. We needed to show superiority against these fuckers, and we did, and we won." The major pauses and takes a long look at the burning fire in his fireplace. "No more unprovoked aggression, Captain, you hear me?" the major asks. Somehow, he is even more imposing with his voice reined in.

The captain slaps his arms against the sides of his body. "Yes sir!"

"We are the U.S. Army. Our government has signed treaties with these Indians, and we will do our best to keep our part of the bargain, you hear me?" asks the major.

"Yes sir!" replies the captain.

"We will escort these people up to their new god-forsaken land and leave them there. They can rot for all I care, but our job is to get them there! Do you understand?"

"Yes sir!" replies the captain.

The major begins to look around his desk again. "You, however, will not be joining the caravan."

The captain's mouth drops. He is surprised and gestures to say something.

The Major sees him though and stops him before he can speak. "Nope, I don't want to hear it. I have made different preparations for you, sir."

"But…" the captain begins to speak, but is once again interrupted.

"I don't trust your character, Captain. You cannot restrain yourself. I suspect that if you were to be in charge of the caravan as planned, there would be no Indians left to escort at the end of the journey."

The captain looks at the major in disbelief.

"Your orders are to return to Fort Charlotte, South Carolina, where your career began. Your Indian days are over," says the major.

"Sir, if I may…" the captain says.

The major finds the paper he is looking for, takes out a small bottle of ink, retrieves his pen, and begins to sign the document, ignoring the captain.

"Sir, excuse me…" says the captain again.

"What?" asks the major, looking up at him in anger.

"The fact that their numbers have thinned…makes them easier to escort. You should be… thanking me, sir," explains the captain.

The major shakes his head, enraged by the captain. He picks up the document he signed, looks at the captain, crumbles it up and throws it at him. The paper hits the captain's forehead, then falls on the floor.

"Get out of my sight! Get out before I change my mind and have you court marshaled for not following orders! Pick up your orders and get out!" says the major.

The captain picks up his orders, but accidentally drops them.

"Out," says the major.

"Yes sir," replies the captain as he picks up his orders again, then drops them again.

"Out!" the major raises his voice again.

The captain picks up his orders, quickly salutes the major and as he scrambles to open the door he drops his gloves.

"You imbecile. You can't even follow a simple order to leave!" yells the major, as the captain picks up his gloves, opens the door and quickly exits. The major stands in his cabin looking at the door as he shakes his head. He looks out the window and sees the light of day fading in the sky, then he sits back on his chair and looks at his desk filled with paperwork and sighs.

Chapter 2: Two Paths

Night falls on the fort. It's a clear night, and a full moon is out as the few remaining clouds in the sky slowly drift away. Lightning bugs fly all around the tall grasses surrounding the camp. As moonlight shines down and brightens the fort, coyotes can be heard in the distance. High up in the trees, toward the rear of the camp, close to the fort wall, there is movement in the leaves. A large owl suddenly flies from one of the branches and into the night, frightened by the subtle noises Tula makes.

She moves effortlessly through the tree branches as she approaches the fort. From tree to tree she jumps until she draws right up against the outside of the encampment wall. Tula slowly balances herself on a tree branch that reaches a small gap in the wall leading to the second floor of one of the cabins that holds the natives. Tula looks around. The guards watching the perimeter are nowhere to be seen. She places her head right up against the hole and can look in through the gap in the large wooden wall beams.

As she peers in, she sees some of the members of her tribe inside of what looks to be a dimly lit cabin room. Some of them sleep covered in blankets, while others sit by the fireplace in silence. There are food scraps on the table in the corner, and two gas lamps that dimly light the room. Tula sees Isi sleeping on the floor, and her eyes fill up with tears. She tries to say something but chokes instead. She is so full of emotion that she must wait and gather herself before speaking. She tries again,

"Psst… *Psst,*" says Tula.

One of the women sitting by the fire hears Tula. She turns around slowly and looks in her direction. The woman gets up, puts a blanket over her shoulders and approaches the wall. The woman recognizes Tula and smiles. Tula puts her little fingers through the gap in the wall, the woman grabs them and kisses them repeatedly and begins to cry. Tula points to Isi sleeping on the floor. The woman turns to look and understands. She nods and takes a few steps toward Isi and whispers,

"Isi… Isi, come!"

Isi stirs a bit, then turns her head to look at the woman beckoning to her. She looks past the woman and catches a glimpse of Tula's face from the hole in the wall. She quickly gets up and runs to her in tears. Isi reaches through and touches her sister as she weeps.

"Tula, I thought they killed you," Isi says.

"I'm here sis. I'm right here…" Tula replies as the girls touch each other's hands through the hole and cry.

Everyone in the cabin has awakened, and they look at Isi and Tula. Nobody makes a sound.

"How did you get up here? It's so high up," says Isi.

"I waited until the guards walked by, then climbed one of those trees back there and made my way through the canopy to find you. I was hoping you were her. I wanted to make sure you were safe… I saw that big man take you," Tula says.

"I'm alive. I'm ok… But a lot of our people have been killed Tula," says Isi.

"I walked through the camp. I know," Tula replies.

Some of the people in the room begin to weep, as they remember the massacre at the camp. Isi looks into the room, and wipes her tears, putting on a show of strength before she looks at Tula again.

She turns to Tula and says, "Mother is gone." She cannot help herself and breaks out into a deep snuffle.

Tula holds her hand and whispers,

"I know… But we still have each other."

A native man resting by the fire climbs to his feet, and quickly goes to the locked cabin door. He puts his ear up against it and whispers to the two girls.

"Be quiet, you'll bring attention!"

The girls gather themselves, trying to stop crying. Isi looks at the man and nods in approval. The man goes back and sits by the fireplace.

Isi turns her attention to Tula and says, "We are migrating north tomorrow; the soldiers are taking us."

"Tomorrow? That is so soon. I don't want you to leave me!" Tula replies.

Isi tries to grab more of Tula's hand but is not able to due to the small size of the gap between the wooden beam walls.

"When…when we leave this encampment tomorrow, follow us from a distance. Keep an eye on me as to where I will be. Then, when we stop to rest somewhere join me, as if you had been with me the whole time. If we are careful, no one will notice," Isi says.

"Nashoba is with me," says Tula.

"Really?" Isi replies as she tries to look outside through the hole in the wall.

"He's not here. He waits for me a distance away," says Tula. "But he does not want to travel north Isi. He says he is old, and wants his bones to remain here, with our ancestors."

There is a short silence as the girls look at each other through the small gap in the wall. A soldier's footsteps can be heard walking up to the door. Isi hears him, looks at the door then looks back at Tula.

"Remember what I said," says Isi as she looks at her little sister's eyes.

"I'll stay hidden and follow you. When you stop to rest, I come out of the woods like I went to the bathroom or something, and join you, as if I had always been traveling with you," Tula says.

Isi nods. She shifts on her heel as she hears a key going into the door lock, and the doorknob begins to turn. She looks back at Tula and says, "Go! Hide!"

Tula vanishes, and Isi slides down the wall, sits, and pretends she's asleep. The door opens, and a young soldier with unkempt hair looks into the room. His eyes are half-closed, and saliva slides down his chin. He looks like he just woke up. He tries to adjust his disheveled uniform as he squints to scrutinized the dimmed lit room.

"Hey…what's going on here?" asks the guard.

The natives say nothing, but stare at the soldier. The soldier yawns, looks around the room and shakes his head.

"I thought I heard someone talking in here. Y'all keep it quiet," says the guard.

"Only one talking…is you," says an old man.

The young guard just stares at him in disdain, and slowly closes the door as he yawns.

All the while, Tula moves away from the fort, through the branches high in the trees, with great speed. She looks for Nashoba in the distance, but he is not where he is supposed to be waiting for her. She glances around and moves up a few branches to get a better look, but suddenly stops. Tula stoops on a thin branch and looks down toward some of the tall grasses in the distance. The moonlight shines on Tula's face. She is concerned as she sees Nashoba crouching down, and slowly moving away from a soldier patrol that is coming toward him.

Nashoba looks up and sees Tula in the trees. He smiles and motions for her to stay where she is at. As the soldiers draw closer, the old man begins to move again, this time a little faster in order to stay ahead of them. He carefully places his feet down and does not make a sound as he moves, but the soldiers walk at a fast pace.

The soldiers stop. One of them lights up a cigarette. They begin to talk, but Tula can't really hear them. Nashoba is no more than a few feet away from them, and as they begin to move again, one of them decides to push the other playfully. They're almost on top of Nashoba.

Tula quickly stands on the branch to get a better look.

Crack!

The branch underneath her breaks, Tula falls, and hits the back of her head as she passes the branches on her way down.

Everything goes black.

*   *   *

The sun is high in the sky now. Amidst a very large, wooded area, amongst trees, tall grasses and wild brush, smoke rises from different fires lit throughout the migrant camp. A light breeze sways the tree branches from side to side. It's a warm clear day. On the wide dirt trail below, the caravan made up of thousands of Choctaw and U.S. soldiers eat ease into a respite. Wagons and horses have been put to rest for the moment underneath the tree canopy on the sides of the trail.

The soldiers sit in their own group, away from the natives, though single-guard patrols walk the perimeter of the group and keep a watchful eye. The soldiers eat and drink. They are well-stocked and even have a cook amongst them that has prepared them lunch: beans, bacon and a slice of bread all around.

The natives, on the other hand, are keeping a tight eye on their rations. Traveling with what little they have, they share amongst themselves. Some of them were not prepared for this journey, having been put into this caravan by force.

Isi is one of those unfortunate ones who is unprepared. She sits by one of the fires, amongst a dozen or so natives from other families. Chewing on a large piece of salted meat, she anxiously looks around for Tula, who was supposed to meet her at her first stop. She looks around and sees soldiers beginning to get up and pack their belongings. She stands up and looks all around. She walks toward the edge of the trail and looks straight into the woods. She does not see her sister.

Isi quickly walks to the other side of the dirt trail, as natives help each other up, and pack their belongings. She looks on this side of the trail but does not see Tula there either. She nervously looks around the camp, and little by little everyone begins to rise.

Fear grips her heart. *Did she miss her?* Isi begins to wonder.

As everyone stirs to move, some of them are putting out their fires, other gathering their belongings, walking toward their horses, packing their things back up into the wagons. Officers bark orders to their soldiers, and the soldiers to the natives.

Isi walks through the multitude of people up the trail, looking to both sides of the trail and into the woods to see if she catches a glimpse of her sister, but she doesn't see her anywhere.

"Where are you Tula?" Isi whispers.

As she continues to walk and look for Tula, she calls out her name. "Tula! Tula where are you!" Isi yells but receives no answer.

She gets to the very front of the party and is stopped by a soldier watching the front.

He puts his hand on her shoulder and says, "We're fixing to get going soon, just get back to the group."

Tula stands to the side and looks in all directions, searching people's faces, looking for her sister.

People are on the move, some people on foot, and some on horseback, returning to the trail. Natives pass her as she stands there looking on, refusing to accept that her sister has not shown up.

A soldier on horseback passes Isi and gives her a dirty look.

A native man sees the soldier and quickly walks to Tula, touches her arms and says, "Let's move now… You cannot just stand here."

Isi turns around and asks him, "Have you seen my sister? She's younger than me. She's supposed to be here, her name is Tula."

"I don't know… There are so many people, here she could be anywhere. But we must move now," says the man. He looks around and begins to walk away.

A soldier walks by Isi, and shoves her on her shoulder, yelling, "Let's go!"

Isi looks at the soldier, ignoring him as people continue to pass her by. Isi turns to the woods again and looks to see if she can find her sister.

"Tula! Tula where are you!" Isi yells, as more and more people pass her by.

A soldier on horseback passing by brushes up against Isi with his horse, spilling her to her hands and knees.

"Let's go woman! Stop standing around!"

The soldier grips the reins, pulling back his horse, and as he watches Isi on the ground, he reaches for a whip on the side of his saddle. Isi sits back on her feet as she looks at the scrapes on her hands. The soldier holds the whip out, and lets it extend down to the ground.

"You better stand up and get to walking, or I'ma whip the shit outta ya," says the soldier.

Before he can do anything else, a young man on horseback rides up and positions his horse in between Isi and the soldier.

Jean Levine is a white man that has joined the caravan. Clad in frontiersmen attire, with pelts sewn together from different types of animals, Jean hops down from the horse's saddle, and quickly moves to stand next to the girl. Jean has long, curly brown hair, a short beard, green eyes and a fair complexion. Isi looks up and sees him standing there smiling at her as he holds out his hand to her. He's wearing some indigenous jewelry that catches her eye. When she looks down at his boots, they look like something a native man would wear. Who is this man, she wonders.

Jean holds out his other hand to the soldier and smiles at him, trying to evoke a bit of patience from him. "I'll get her up sir. I'll make sure she complies! She probably does not understand a word you're saying," laughs Jean.

"She'll understand my fucking whip across her back!" the soldier replies.

Jean leans down, grabs Isi's elbows, and helps her stand up. The soldier continues to watch, whip in hand. He slightly flicks his wrist, letting a quick snap echo from the end of the whip.

"Come with me, or this will not end well for you," says Jean in Choctaw.

Isi is surprised as she looks into Jean's eyes. She quickly dusts herself off, with Jean helping her to brush the dust off her back.

Jean walks to his horse quickly and tells the soldier, "See, no harm done. We're on our way!" He looks at Isi and smiles. After he climbs on his horse, he reaches out with his hand and says in Choctaw, "Come on…take my hand. Let me get you out of here, quickly. Come on! This soldier is not playing around."

Isi takes Jean's hand and gets on his horse under the watchful eye of the soldier. Jean nudges his horse, and they begin to move with the rest of the people, as everyone now seems to be on the go. The soldier rides beside Jean, nods, and rides away, forward into the crowd of natives.

"Are you hurt? Need some water?" asks Jean, as he holds out his canteen out to her.

Isi takes the canteen and draws a long sip from it. She taps Jean with it on the shoulder. He takes it back and puts it in the saddlebag.

"What's going on? Why were you just standing at the side of the trail?" asks Jean

Isi looks around and sees that nobody is paying attention to them anymore. Everyone is preoccupied with their own things, minding their own business.

"I was looking for my sister. She was supposed to join me at midday... She never showed up," says Isi.

"You mean...she did not depart with you?" asks Jean.

Isi gazes into the woods as they ride, hoping to maybe see Tula waving back at her. "No, we got separated," says Isi.

She continues to look around but sees only strangers. The caravan is vast. Isi looks forward and sees that there are hundreds of natives in front of them, and when she looks back, hundreds more. Some people are on horseback, some have wagons, and many are on foot. They all carry everything they own with them, their whole lives uprooted. Now they are in the process of being transplanted to an unknown land. The spirit of sadness and defeat hangs strongly over them all, evident on every face, from the babies to the adults. The heaviness of every heart is so evident, each of them carries the weight of a world of pain. The reality of what is happening hits Isi hard, and tears begin to fall from her eyes.

"So, when did you last see your sister? What is her name?" asks Jean.

Isi dries her tears, and tries to be strong for the stranger as she replies, "I saw her back at the soldier fort last night. She said she would be here. It's not like her! Tula likes to play around, but this is different… Where is that girl?"

"Well, my name is…" Jean begins to say but is quickly interrupted by Isi.

"Maybe she's back at the fort. Maybe she's in trouble! "

"They won't let you go back; no one leaves this group until we get to where we're going. By the way, my name is…" replies Jean, but as he tries to introduce himself, Isi interrupts again.

"She's got to be back there…"

Isi knocks Jean from his horse and takes command of it. Jean is able to adjust his fall so he lands on his hand and knees. He quickly turns around and looks up, but Isi is gone, a dust trail leading in the direction she urges the horse onward to. She quickly disappears amidst the travelers.

Isi rides toward the back of the migration, passing natives and soldiers alike. Everyone's eyes are on her now as she weaves the horse from side to side to avoid colliding with anyone.

"Tula! Tula where are you!" Isi yells as she rides and desperately looks around for her sister.

A sergeant riding with a group of soldiers sees Isi race past him. He looks at his soldiers and points back at her and says, "Stop that girl!"

Two soldiers on horseback immediately give chase. Isi looks back and sees them coming after her, but she does not care. She is determined to find Tula. She rides past wagons, and multitudes of people on foot, creating a wake of startled people as she passes by. Some soldiers see her coming and try to position their horses in her way to stop her, but she cuts into the woods, and then comes back to the edge of the trail as she makes her way back. Those soldiers also begin to chase after her.

People jump out of her way, and wagons steer from her path as Isi tries to stay ahead of the soldiers behind her now. Finally, Isi sees the end of the migration party, and it's all soldiers—most of them on wagons and on horseback. The soldiers see her coming a far way off. The trail of dirt she picks up is like a waving flag alerting everybody of her approach. The soldiers pick up their rifles and pistols and point at her as she approaches. Isi sees the firing squad in front of her and slows the horse down in fear. She brings the horse to a stop and raises her hands.

One of the soldiers atop one of the wagons stands up and says, "Where the hell do you think you're going?"

The sergeant that she passed earlier catches up to her with the rest of the soldiers. He grabs Is by her shirt, smacks her and pulls her off the horse, and onto his. Bringing her face before his, he says, "No one leaves, woman. What is going on with you?"

"Let me take care of her, Sarge!" one of the soldiers says, receiving a smile from the officer. The soldier grabs Isi by her hair and roughly pulls her head backward to take a better look at her. "We can definitely have some fun, Sarge!" says the soldier.

Jean suddenly rides up to them on the back of a native man's horse, screaming out loud. "Wait! Wait a minute please!"

The native man stops his horse in front of the soldiers, and Jean jumps off, quickly approaching the sergeant with arms up in the air.

"Gentlemen, there seems to be a big misunderstanding here," says Jean.

The sergeant lets go of Isi. She slides down his horse onto the ground and runs to Jean. All eyes dart to Jean as he gives them a charming smile and places the girl behind him.

"Ah…Mr. Lavigne, of course. Please do elaborate. Enlighten us on this situation before I have to do something about this soldier's lack of restraint," says the sergeant.

"This girl is simply looking for her lost sister. She…uh…borrowed my horse to go and look for her. It seems to me that she may have lost control of the horse."

"Seems to me she's an excellent rider—better than most of my men!" the sergeant replies.

"Sure is. Better than you, Sarge!" says one of the soldiers.

"Quiet!" yells the sergeant, who then continues. "You were saying, Mr. Lavigne?"

"I do apologize, Sergeant, for all the commotion. She was just a little lost. No harm done? If you would allow me, I will take her back with me and we can continue on our journey? With your permission of course," says Jean.

The sergeant looks at Jean for a few seconds and then looks over at Isi, hiding behind him. He then glances at his soldiers, like wolves ready to pounce. "Fine! You take the woman with you. She is now your responsibility. No more excitement for today, Mr. Lavigne, or any other day, you hear? And let's be on our way!"

Jean nods and says, "Thank you. Thank you, Sergeant!"

He mounts his horse, and pulls Isi up to him, situating her in front of him. Together, they ride up to join the group of people walking ahead.

Isi holds the back of the saddle, leans forward, and says, "Thank you… So, what was your name?"

Jean smiles slightly and shakes his head. They are again surrounded by the sea of people migrating north.

*   *   *

A distance away, Tula slowly opens her eyes. Dazed and confused, she gently puts her hand to the back of her head, where she was struck by the tree branch as she fell. There is a large bump there. She pulls her hand away; it hurts to touch.

Her body rocks back and forth suddenly, and she realizes she's on a moving wagon. As she continues to come to, she hears horses moving, and men talking all around her. She slowly sits up, rubs her eyes with the heels of her hands, and sees herself sitting on a pile of hay. She looks around and is surprised to see that she's in an open-caged wagon.

Beautiful cumulous clouds above are moved by a gentle breeze, revealing a deep blue sky behind them. The sunrays fall through the leaves of the trees to the right and left of the trail the wagon travels on. Birds chirp and sing from all sides. Tula looks up as she hears the cry of an eagle in the distance. She looks around, and through the bars of the wagon, she sees armed men on horseback—one on either side of the wagon, and two in the back.

She looks to the front of the wagon and sees that she is not alone. There are black people in the wagon with her: a young girl a little older than Tula, four women and two young men. They all gather together toward the front of the wagon, crouched down, looking at Tula in fear.

This is a slave wagon.

Tula looks back at the men riding behind the wagon. They have been eying her up carefully.

"Well, take a look-a here Sam… Redskin's finally awake," says Jimmy, a simpleton slaver with rotten teeth. Wearing overalls and no shoes, he looks like he should be on a farm.

"Ha! After two days, she just pops up, just like that. You think we'll get anything for her Jimbo?" says Sam, a slaver from Georgia, dressed in what remains of a white suit, with shoes so worn you can see the bottom of his feet through the soles.

"I don't know. We'll find something to do with her," says Jimmy.

Tula tries to stand but hits her head on the top bars of the cage, eliciting laughs from Jimmy. She holds onto the bars, and stumbles over to the right side of the wagon. Tula reaches out to the rider on that side and pleads for help, "Please mister, I need to find my sister. I should not be here…"

The fat man on horseback rides a little bit closer to the cage, smiling at her as he does. Then when he draws close enough, he spits a glob of tobacco and saliva right on her face and says,

"Shut up! I can't understand a word you're saying, little monkey-in-a-cage."

"Ha! Damn, you covered her whole face with that shit there, Danny!" says Jimmy.

Danny, a tall black-haired, skinny fellow dressed in multiple layers of clothing to compensate for his thin frame. Some people claim he is from the Caribbean, but he insists he is from Spain.

Tula spits—as some of the tobacco got in her mouth—and wipes her face with her forearm.

When she looks at Danny, he says, "Te voy a filetear, monita"

"What did he say?' asks Jimmy

"You don't want to know," says Bobby from the other side of the wagon.

Tula turns around and sees Bobby, blond-haired and blue-eyed. He is a young, good-looking fellow, dressed in mostly black. He looks back at Tula and smiles. Tula quickly moves to his side of the wagon and reaches out to him, her arm fully extended, hoping that he would have some pity.

Bobby rides his horse close to the wagon and allows Tula's hand to touch his face, her fingertips brushing against his cheek.

Tula smiles and thinks that he is being nice. Maybe this man will help her, she thinks. But then Bobby takes her hand into his mouth and begins to lick it. Tula does not understand, and quickly pulls away. Bobby sticks out his tongue out at her and flicks it up and down as he rubs his crotch. Tula squirms toward the front of the wagon with the others.

"Oh boy. You've done it now, redskin! Bobby's got his eye on you …" says Jimmy.

Bobby continues to rub himself as he blows kisses at Tula. Sam looks at Bobby as he continues to carry on and says, "I haven't seen Bobby this excited since we found that little black girl in that basket. What was that, almost a year ago now? I can't believe what he did to that thing! Bobby, you knew she was money!"

"Wha…what did he do?" asks Jimmy.

"Well, you weren't with us then. About a year or so ago, we was called to do a transport. They had found some runaways in this man's house; they were all hiding in the basement. They found some in storage cabinets, others in potato sacks, and no-one knew where they had come from—about nine of 'em. It was assumed they had escaped from another wagon carrying them to the auction house from the docks. After we got 'em all loaded up, and we sent the wagon on its way, boss tells Bobby to take one final look at the house, then meet us back at the auction house…" says Sam, then he takes a look at Bobby ridding his horse.

"What happened next?" asks Jimmy. He presses again soon after. "Well? What happened?'

Sam looks over at Jimmy with a glossed-over, stoic face and says, "Bobby never did make it back to the auction house, we went looking for him the next morning and found him in that basement fucking what remained of a slave child," said Sam.

Jimmy looks over at Bobby, disturbed at what he's hearing. He looks over at Danny, who is already looking back at him and smiling.

"He fucked her right in half," says Danny.

"Wha…?" says Jimmy, then looks over at Bobby, who is ignoring the conversation, just looking at the trees. Jimmy then looks over at Sam again, who nods as he continues.

"We found Bobby asleep in a corner with a little black torso wrapped around his cock—no legs; no arms. When we woke him up, he said he didn't remember anything. And guess what. We only found one of the legs…"

"What?" asks Jimmy.

"Yup… We think he ate the other one since his lips had dried blood on 'em when we found him," says Sam.

"And then?" asks Jimmy.

Sam looks at him, offering a nonchalant expression. "Then nothin'. We got Bobby up, cleaned him up, and a pig farmer that lived nearby fed the remains to his pigs. Nothin' to it."

"Well shit," says Jimmy as he looks over at Bobby, who is sends a wink his way.

Bobby turns around and looks over at Tula, blows her a kiss and smiles creepily.

Tula slides over to the other slaves a she looks at Bobby. The young African girl moves over to Tula and hugs her, Tula hugs her back. Tula looks at the young girl and notices the dried blood on her torn dress, as well as a deep black eye. The girls hug for a little while, and then they slowly pull away and look at each other as they sit on the hay.

"My name is Abeke," says Abeke as she puts her hand on her chest and speaks in the Choctaw tongue.

Tula smiles and nods. She puts her hand on her own chest and says, "Tula… Tula."

Abeke slightly smiles, nods her head and says, "Hello Tula."

"Hello Abeke." says Tula.

Abeke takes Tula's hand and places it on the palm of her own hand. She looks down at their hands, then peers into Tula's eyes and says, "I'm glad to meet you Tula. Maybe we can be friends?"

"I would like that," says Tula. "How do you know my tongue?"

Abeke looks at Tula for a few seconds, then says, "It's a long story, another time maybe…"

Tula, holding Abeke's hand, sits back against the iron bars on the side of the wagon, Abeke sitting beside her. Tula looks at Abeke and puts her arm around her. Abeke's eyes swell with tears that begin to the slowly drop down her cheeks. Tula holds Abeke's shoulder and brings her a bit closer to herself.

"I guess we're prisoners, but at least we're together," says Tula.

They travel all afternoon, across the dusty road. Tula, Abeke and the rest of the slaves do not say a word, but the slavers mock them and joke as they carry on their conversations.

Day turns into dusk, and beneath tall bold cypress trees and water tupelos the slave wagon comes to a rough stop, close to the water's edge. The last bit of daylight quickly fades in the sky, giving way to thousands of stars. Frogs and insects of every type can be heard singing in the area. Plops and an occasional splash are heard coming from the water as critters move in the lagoon the group comes to rest beside. The driver of the wagon jumps down and walks toward the back. Peter Landonman is his name. The son of a slaver, he has been a slaver all his life. The short, long-haired little man, dressed in yellow slacks and a shirt too fancy to be on the road with, walks up to Bobby and clears his throat.

"Alright, Bobby. Let's git a camp goin' here. Why don't you go ahead and fetch some firewood fo' us."

Bobby looks at him with disappointment and replies, "Well, who's gonna take care them slaves Pete? "

"Don't you worry about that. Gon' get some wood now!"

Bobby gets off his horse disappointed, murmuring something under his breath as he slowly walks away. Jimmy and Sam come around from the back of the wagon, already off their horses. Sam takes the reins of Bobby's horse and Jimmy's and walks them to one of the large trees to tie them up.

Bobby speaks loud enough in the woods for everyone to hear him. "Bobby, get the wood… Bobby, get some water… Bobby, feed the horses!"

Pete hears him and shakes his head. He points to the slave wagon and says, "You boys get them slaves off that wagon and secure them to that tree over there. I don't want them shitting in the wagon. Make sure them chains are tight now."

"Will do, senor," says Danny. "Hey, Jimmy, help me out."

As Sam secures the horses a short distance away, Danny takes a large ring with keys from his pocket and throws it at Jimmy, who opens a chest beside the wagon filled with chains and fetters. Danny gets his rifle from his shoulder and points it at the slaves as Jimmy unlocks the door.

"Alright, you know the drill," Jimmy says. "Come on out slowly and let me put these on ya."

One by one the slaves step out of the wagon and are chained up together. Tula is hesitant to step out.

Jimmy looks at her and shakes the chains and says, "If I have to come get you, I promise you're not gonna like it. Let's go!"

Abeke slightly nudges her to go and Tula steps out and allows herself to be shackled. She looks back at Abeke and sees her stand up for the first time and is surprised to see that Abeke is with child.

Sam comes back to the wagon and says, "I'ma take these boys and these women right here and we'll set up camp. Danny, come with me."

"Sounds good. I'll take the little Indian and her friend. They'll help me make supper," says Peter.

Jimmy pushes Tula and Abeke in Peter's direction. Peter takes their chains and leads them to the front of the wagon.

Bobby comes out of the woods holding a big pile of wood. He sees the girls being led by Peter, drops everything, points at them and says, "Hey! Why am I the only one working alone! Pete, let me get one of them girls to help me with the wood here!"

Peter waves his hand at Bobby, shaking his head enthusiastically. "No way. No way, Bobby! You keep your hands off these girls! You hear me? Them is money, not for touching."

Bobby grabs his crotch and thrusts forward a few times at the girls. He kicks a piece of wood on the ground and walks back into the woods.

Dusk turns to night, and the pale moonlight shines down upon the camp lighting up the clouds, the top of the trees, and the lagoon nearby. A small campfire illuminates the nearby area, as bats fly back and forth, eating the flying insects drawn by the light of the fire. The slavers have settled down, and seem to be asleep, close to the fire.

Tula, Abeke and the other slaves are back in the wagon, set a couple of yards away from camp, close to the horses. They are all eating scraps from a bucket. Abeke pulls a chicken bone from the bucket and gives it to Tula.

"How can you live off these bones?" asks Tula.

"It's better than living off nothing, and I've done that already, so go ahead and chew it good," says Abeke.

"Where are these men taking us?" asks Tula.

Abeke reaches down into the bucket, but there is nothing left. The last bone was taken by one of the boys in the wagon. She sits down, looks at the boy with the bone in his mouth, then makes eye contact with Tula. "We're gonna get sold and sent to work somewhere," she says.

Tula looks at Abeke and points to her belly.

"They'll take the baby and sell that too, like a piece of meat in the market," says Abeke.

Tula sits back on the side of the wagon and contemplates as tears begin to fall down her face. Abeke sits beside her, and they look at the moonlight shining on the lagoon, and the dwindling, fading fire of the camp.

"The white devils took all of our land, killed hundreds—thousands of my people," Tula says. "And they said it was all for peace. No… I'm not going to be sold. I'm going to leave… I have to find my sister." Tula reaches out and places her hand over Abeke's hand and says, "Will you come with me?"

Abeke slowly nods her head in approval. Then, suddenly, a noise in the bushes catches her attention. Tula also hears it, and she also looks. The rumbling in the bushes seems to be coming toward them, and they get on their hands and knees and crouch with expectation. As the noises draw closer and closer, they slowly begin to move backward. Then, out of nowhere, Bobby comes out of the bushes, smiling. Tula and Abeke quickly move to the front of the wagon, waking up the other slaves.

Bobby walks right up to the wagon bars, his eyes fixated on Tula. And like a wolf salivating over its prey, Bobby smiles creepily, and licks his lips. He takes a piece of beef jerky out of his pocket and holds it up for Tula to see. He smiles wider, waves it in the air and whispers to the girl. "*Redskin,*" his quiet voice elongates the word into disturbing musical notes. I know you want this, redskin."

He breaks a piece of it off and holds it out for Tula to take. The girl looks at him with distrust, but she slowly moves a little bit closer to him. She quickly snatches the piece from his hand.

Bobby giggles and says, "You're alright… I got more for you if you want it."

Tula takes a bite of the beef and hands it to Abeke, who eats the rest. Tula watches the young man carefully.

Bobby continues to giggle. He holds the rest of the beef jerky up in the air and slowly puts it in his front shirt pocket. He steps even closer to the cage bars and looks in. Everyone in the wagon tries to move away from him as they gather at the front of the wagon. Bobby reaches into his back pocket and pulls out a large, bundled cloth. He loosens it and throws it into the wagon. The bundle opens up mid air and beef jerky flies everywhere. The slaves scramble to get as much as they can, except for Tula, who watches him carefully.

"I need y'all to shut up for a little bit. This will keep your mouths busy," laughs Bobby.

He looks over at Tula, pulls out the piece of beef that was in his front pocket, and holds it out to her, but Tula is not moving—she just stares at him. Bobby reaches down to his belt, and unhooks a ring of keys, finding a particular one as he looks over at the campsite. He sees that all the other slavers are fast asleep. He looks back at Tula, and slowly unlocks the wagon door. Bobby inches into the wagon and holds the beef closer to Tula's face to entice her. Tula is so hungry, she can't resist and reaches for it. Bobby snatches her wrist and begins to pull her. Tula holds on to the bars of the wagon, but her hands slip. Bobby is too strong for her. Abeke sees Tula being pulled away and grabs her shoulders, trying to pull her back into the wagon while Tula tries to grab another iron bar.

"Leave her alone! Let her go!" Abeke yells.

Bobby punches Abeke in the face, knocking her backward. With one more pull, he grabs Tula and holds her tight underneath his chin, covering her mouth so she does not yell. Bobby slowly closes the door to the cage, looks

into Abeke's eyes and says, "Shh… We won't be long.
Make any noises and I'll come back and eat ya!" Bobby
giggles as he quickly walks away from the wagon and into
the woods with Tula.

Abeke rocks back and forth in desperation. She
looks to one side. All the slavers are asleep. If she wakes
them, what would they do? She thinks to herself about
whether they would even care? Abeke looks at the other
slaves, and they just stare at her in fear. She goes to the
other side of the wagon and looks in the direction that
Bobby entered the woods. Upset, she grabs the bars of the
wagon tightly and silently screams as she looks down to the
ground, and to her shadow inside of the wagon's shadow.
As she looks at the shadows, she notices something in the
darkness, and almost can't believe it. She quickly goes to
the door, puts her arm out and feels for the lock. Bobby left
the keys in the lock!

*   *   *

Meanwhile, in a small grassy clearing in the woods,
lit up by moonlight, Bobby comes out of the forest, holding

Tula, who is struggling to wriggle free from him. Bobby takes a rope that's attached to his belt, puts a noose around Tula's neck, and lets her go.

Tula immediately runs, but as she tries to take the rope off, her captor quickly jerks the rope, yanking her to the ground.

Bobby laughs. He quickly runs to Tula and holds her up by the rope with one hand, her feet barely touching the ground. He begins to rip her clothes off. Tula tries to resist, but he's too strong for her and easily overpowers her. Bobby laughs and giggles as he begins to undo his trousers. He throws Tula on the ground and pins her with the weight of his body, as he holds the rope with one hand and continues to try to undo his pants.

Tula cries. She struggles to free herself to no avail. She closes her eyes and surrenders to her fate, tensing up as she waits for this terror to unravel upon her. She grimaces in fear, but after a few seconds, to her surprise, nothing happens. Bobby has stopped moving, and as she opens her eyes, she looks Bobby's face, seeing a wooden branch sticking out of his eye socket, blood dripping down on her forehead.

Tula traces the shape of the stick with her eyes, and as she looks around Bobby's head, she sees Abeke holding the other end of it as she stands over them with an expression of fury on her face.

"Abeke!" Tula says, but Abeke does not answer. She is enraged still. "Abeke, help me get up," says Tula again.

Abeke lets go of the stick. She quickly squats and pushes Bobby's body up enough for Tula to slide out. Abeke stands and looks at Bobby's face with the stick coming out of the eye socket, then she looks over at Tula, standing there naked looking back at her.

"He was gonna kill you after, you know," says Abeke.

Tula reaches out, grabs Abeke, and hugs her tightly. Abeke hugs her back. As Tula begins to cry and shake, the realization of what could have happened takes hold of her. Abeke holds her for a few more minutes.

Finally, Tula begins to calm down. She takes a deep breath and nods to Abeke. "I have a new sister today… Thank you."

Abeke softly lets her go, and says, "We have to find your clothes."

The girls walk around the area picking up pieces of what's left of her clothes. Bobby tore them to shreds.

Tula holds up the rags she's picked up and says, "There's no way I can put this back on"

Abeke nods in understanding, and as she's looking around, an idea manifests, with a smile quickly following. She hurries to Bobby's body, puts her foot on his head and pulls the large stick out of his head. She turns him over, begins to unbutton his shirt and looks over at Tula. Tula understands immediately, runs to Abeke, and begins to help her undress the body. Tula takes his belt off and unbuttons his trousers. Abeke pulls them off his body. In just a few minutes, Tula is dressed in Bobby's clothing, Tula takes his knife, and puts it on her hip, right on her new belt.

"Let me see that knife please," asks Abeke.

Tula hands her the knife, Abeke takes it and cuts the sleeves off the shirt. Tula smiles—she likes what's happening here. Abeke then proceeds to cut off the bottom of the pant legs. Just as she finishes making the cut, the girls hear a big commotion coming from the slaver camp. They both looks in that direction, surprised, and terrified.

They hear screaming, and yelling. There are many noises, and then a gunshot rings out. Suddenly, one of the horses gallops out of the woods, and into the clearing. The girls flinch after standing frozen in fear for so long. The horse slowly comes up to them and nudges them with his mouth.

Abeke looks at Tula and tries to tun back to the camp, but Tula quickly stops her.

"If we don't go back, they will find us, and then it will be a lot worse!" says Abeke.

Tula points at Bobby's body and says, "They will find his body, and then we're both dead…"

"So we run?" asks Abeke.

Tula walks over to the horse, grabs it by the mane, and jumps on his back in one go. Tula pats the horse on the neck, looks over at Abeke and says,

"No. We ride!"

Abeke runs to Tula, grabbing her extended arm to climb onto the horse. Noises are coming from the woods behind them. It's obvious that someone is coming. Tula kicks the horse, and the girls disappear into the woods.

A few minutes later, Jimmy comes out of the woods, rifle in hand. Visibly angry, he walks around in the clearing until he sees Bobby's naked body on the ground. He slowly walks over to Bobby, and nudges him with his foot. It is then that he sees the grisly wound in the lad's head. He squats down to get a closer look and says, "Looks like you finally got yours Bobby…you ignant fool!"

Jimmy gets up and looks back in the direction of the camp. "Hey! I found Bobby over here!" he yells.

*   *   *

Hours go by, and beneath a deep blue sky, the rays of the morning sun slowly begin to shine over the top of the thick forest canopy. The sunlight hits the opposite side of the river tree line, where birds sing, and a few rabbits wander through the tall grasses by the river's edge. A single deer walks out of the forest, puts its head down to grab some grass, then quickly raises its head and hears something. He quickly runs away.

Suddenly, Tula and Abeke burst out of the forest on horseback and stop short by the river's edge, sending all the rabbits and birds scattering in fear. The horse is covered in sweat and breathes heavily. Tula, in good command of the horse, walks it to the river's edge and climbs off. She reaches up and helps Abeke get off the horse as well, cupping her pregnant belly.

As the horse begins to drink water, Tula looks at Abeke and says, "We should drink as well. Go ahead…"

Tula helps Abeke reach the water's edge. Abeke kneels and brings cupped hands filled with water up to her mouth to sate her thirst. Tula looks around for a little while, checking to see if they are being followed or not, but sees nothing but trees, their branches swaying to a soft breeze that passes by. The wind changes and she catches the scent of what's coming out of the forest. Everything seems to be clear for now. She joins Abeke by the riverside, kneels and puts her face right down to the water to drink as she looks around.

Abeke takes a few steps in, and squats down in the water. She begins to pour water on her neck and arms, sighing as she lets off some of the stress from the previous night. As she does, a few feet away by a large boulder in the river, she sees a few fish swimming around. Abeke looks over at Tula, who is already standing, looking back at her and the fish. Abeke lunges toward the fish, but slips and falls right into the water. Tula walks over to her, laughing, and helps her up before walking her over to a large stone so she can sit down.

"I have an idea," says Tula, eliciting a nod of approval from Abeke.

Tula takes the knife at her hip, walks over to the tree line, and begins to look at the young saplings carefully.

"What are you doing?" asks Abeke, but Tula does not respond and keeps inspecting the trees.

Abeke looks closely as Tula walks from tree to tree until she finds one that is long enough, and traitor enough to her liking. Tula takes the knife and begins to chop it at the base. She then takes the knife and begins to give one of the ends a sharp point. Abeke gets up and walks over to her as she hacks at the end of the pole.

"You're making a spear?" asks Abeke

Tula smiles and nods. She stops for a second and picks up two small rocks, she strikes the together to make sparks and asks,

"Fire—do you know how to make fire?"

"Fire? Yes, I can make a fire," Abeke replies.

Tula points to the fish in the river and says, "Good. I'll go get some fish. Then we eat."

Abeke starts picking up the stick immediately, smiles at Tula and says, "You don't have to tell me twice. That'll be the best meal I've had in a long time!"

*   *   *

Shortly after, the sun has risen a little bit in the sky, its light shines down on both sides of the river as a few clouds move into the firmament above. The girls' horse chews on some tender grasses by the river, as the girls sit by a small fire and suck what meat remains of a fish from the bones in their hands. The spear has one more fish on it. Tula points to it, sending a curious glance toward her friend.

"No, I've had enough for now," Abeke says.

Tula takes a few large leaves, breaks up the fish, wraps it up, and puts it in her pockets. She walks over to the horse and gives it a good pat on the head. She looks up and sees the clouds coming in.

Abeke glances at the sky as well and says, "We've been here too long. We should get going."

Tula looks into the forest again and says, "Yes… We should be going."

"Maybe we should head out further west. We can find new land—new opportunity," says Abeke.

Tula looks into Abeke's eyes for a few seconds considering what she is saying, then replies, "I was supposed to meet my sister on a trail going north, and I missed her. My people are traveling with her, and I have to join her. Will you come with me, new sister?"

Abeke gets up, throws sand on the fire to put it out and walks over to Tula. She puts her hand on her shoulder and says, "Wherever you go, I will be with you. After all, two are better than one."

Tula smiles and says, "Yes, and when we find Isi, we shall be three."

Abeke smiles, gives Tula a hug, then pulls away slightly and says, "Now help me get back on that horse"

Tula points to a small boulder and says, "Stand on that, and I will walk the horse over to you."

As Abeke walks over to the boulder, Tula climbs atop the horse, and walks him over to Abeke.

"How do you make the horse walk, turn and move? You've got no reins" says Abeke.

Tula brings the side of the horse right in front of Abeke, stops it, and helps her mount. "I respect the horse; the horse respects me. I talk to the horse with love, and the horse answers, loves me back." Tula turns around, looks at Abeke, smiles and says, "It's a spiritual thing."

Abeke looks at Tula, a little bit bewildered, and replies, "Uh…ok."

The girls begin to travel north, following the Mississippi River as a guide. They don't see anyone on either side of the river, but stay vigilant, thinking that those slavers may be chasing them. They enjoy each other's company and share a few laughs as the day slowly passes. They stay on the horse and share the fish in Tula's pocket as they travel, stopping briefly from time to time to give some respite to the horse, to Abeke's body, and to drink water or relieve themselves.

*   *   *

Miles away, at the U.S. fort, the sun is setting. Just a little bit of purple and pink in the horizon remain as the light of the sun quickly disappears. On the other end of the sky the stars and moon are already visible. Almost as if they can hardly wait to have their moment, they push the day away. A few birds fly across the front gates of the fort, chirping as they make their way toward the trees.

The slavers with their wagon have reached the outpost. One man short, there is only one slaver in the back, and one on each side the guard the wagon. The slaves, beat up and raggedy, hold onto the bars of the wagon as they travel. They wipe their swollen lips and rub the bruises they received. The slavers look a bit roughed up as well. They all look somber and a bit stoic.

Peter Landonman brings the wagon to a stop, right in front of the fort walls, as he looks up at one of the guards.

"Whoa there!" says Peter to the horses.

The guard up in the tower picks his nose, wipes it on his uniform and says, "What's your business here mister?"

Peter takes his hat off, and puts it to his chest, trying to look as vulnerable as he can and says, "Hello sir. Name's Peter. Peter Landonman. We from the Franklin and Armfield Company. We just passing through taking a shipment o' slaves down t' New Orleans… Auction house."

The guard looks over at the wagon, and the other slavers look up at him. He takes a handkerchief out to wipe the blood from his finger, he blows his bloody nose and says,

"Understood… But why are you here?"

Peter rocks back and forth on the seat of the wagon a little bit. He extends his hand. "Just looking t' spend the night in safety. Not looking for any trouble, sir."

The guard continues to send Peter a reserved look. Unsure if he can trust him, he says, "Well, you guys look like shit. Who's you? You bringing trouble to my door?"

"No, no, no sir. Nothing like that," Peter replies.

"Then what? I can tell something ain't right here!" says the guard.

Peter puts his hat back on and says, "It's a bit embarrassing, but two of our slaves overpowered one of my men. They killed him and ran off with a horse."

"What?" exclaims the guard.

"I know, I know. A terrible business that is. We just need somewhere where we can rest for the night."

"They killed one of your men? When did this happen?" asks the guard.

"They sure did… It happened last night. And we looked for 'em for quite a while through the night and early morning. Unfortunately we couldn't find 'em. But we had to keep goin'. Got a deadline to meet!"

The guard nods his head, looks down at someone below, on the inside of the gate, and says, "Go ahead and open it… Let them in."

The large wooden gates slowly open. A few guards come out and meet the slavers as they stand on either side of the gate. Peter snaps the reins of the wagon, and they enter the fort. The slavers look defeated and beat up.

One of the guards looks at Peter and asks, "So, them slaves must a been pretty big to take down one of your men, him being armed and all, huh?"

"Yes, yes," says Peter.

But before he can continue, one of the slave women points to the guard and says, "Was two little girls, one of 'em pregnant…"

"Shut up back there!" scream Peter in his thick southern accent.

All the guards break out in hysterical laughter. They point and jest as the slavers pass them by, shaming them as they enter the fort.

*   *   *

A little while later, Peter stands in front of one of the cabins within the fort. He looks inside through the front window and sees nothing special. It's just a small cabin with raw wooden posts, a few pictures of soldiers on the wall, and a small, dirty rug by the narrow lit fireplace. A wooden table, a few stools, and a half-lit gas lamp sitting at the edge of the table adorn the place. A little bit of moonlight comes in through the window Peter looks in through and shines on the floor inside. It does not help. He can't see anyone in there, but he does hear the squeaking of a bed, and it must be coming from a room inside.

Peter knocks on the door and suddenly everything becomes still inside. Peter hears the voice of a young man moaning from inside the cabin, but he can't make out what he's saying. Peter knocks on the door again and quickly goes to the window to see if anybody comes to the door.

"Captain, I'm so very sorry to disturb you, this time a night. But If I could please have a few minutes o' yo' time…" Peter yells as he looks through the window.

Peter smiles, as he sees a door to a room at the back of the cabin suddenly slam open. Captain Francis comes out of the back room naked, wiping his penis with a rag as he makes his way to the front door. Peter looks into the back room, and sees a young blonde soldier naked in there, wiping his butt with a small handkerchief.

The captain walks by the wooden table, throws the dirty rag on a stool and picks up a piece of bread from the dirty plate, chewing it as he walks to the door. Peter goes to the door again, and lightly knocks again.

"I'm coming, dam it!" yells the captain.

The captain finally opens the door wide, completely exposing himself without a care in the world. The captain is so tall that his forehead reaches the top of the door frame, and he is so wide, that his shoulders reach the sides of the doorjamb. Peter looks up at the captain, surprised by the red, hairy beast that stands before him, naked and still semi-erect.

The captain looks down at Peter, who is just looking up at him, and says, "Well?""

"Ugh, yes! S…sorry to bother you, sir. I, uh, hope it's not a bad time," Peter says.

"Are you fucking kidding me? Yes, it's a bad time, and yes you are bothering me! You know what time it is, idiot?" asks the captain.

The young soldier that was in the captain's quarters, now almost fully dressed squeezes by the captain and quickly exits the cabin. The captain's glare softens as he looks at the young man leaving. He follows him with his gaze as he walks away. Then he looks back at Peter and his countenance changes to anger. "Well, my night is ruined… The hell do you want?"

Peter turns to look back at the young man walking away into a group of trees, then he looks back at the captain's fiery eyes, forces a smile and says, "I won't be long sir. If I could just have a word?"

"Let me make myself very clear to you sir, when you came to my door you saw the soldier assisting me with administrative paperwork. You interrupted us, and I asked him to leave," the captain says.

"He was just helpin' wit papers," Peter agrees.

"Because if you saw anything else I would have to arrest you and your men, confiscate all your goods, and investigate why it is that you showed up at a military fort with slaves that don't belong to you," says the captain.

"I was just knocking on your door just now. What soldier are you takin 'bout?"

"Good, good…" says the captain. The captain turns around, walks back into his cabin and picks up a pair of trousers from a rocking chair in the corner.

Peter slowly enters the cabin, takes his hat off, and says, "Nice pla—"

"Spit it out. Make it quick! " the captain interrupts. The captain finishes putting on his trousers and sits at the table. Peter closes the door to the cabin, and slowly walks up to the captain. "Well?" asks the captain.

"Yes, uh. You may have heard by now. My crew and I lost…"

"Two fucking girls. They killed one of your men and you're going to sell the remaining slaves in New Orleans. I was briefed," says the captain.

"Yes, yes that's true. And stole one of my best horses too. So…so I'm here with a proposition for you."

The captain reaches for his food on his plate again, picks up a piece of potato with his fingers, looks at Peter and says, "And what might that proposition be?" The captain puts the piece of potato in his mouth and wipes his hand on the rag he used to wipe his penis.

Peter approaches the table, and points to one of the stools. "May I sit down?" he asks.

"No, you may not," replies the captain, as he reaches for another piece of potato.

Peter steps back, straightens out and says, "If you know of a tracker I can hire—someone that is good at finding people…"

The captain gives Peter his full attention now, turning his whole body toward him.

Peter sees this, and quickly walks to the table, takes a stool, sits right in front of the captain and continues. "I need to find the young negro woman. She be with child, and she's very valuable. The other girl, an Indian we picked up, close to the encampment here and…"

Intrigued, the captain leans in toward Peter and asks, "What do you mean, close to the encampment?"

Peter adjusts himself in the stool, and says, "Well…almost 3 days ago, as we was on our way, we was passing this very fort here. Just a few yards away from the southern wall, one of my men found a young Indian girl passed out in the bushes. There were some soldiers nearby. We calls them over, but they were no help. The girl was unconscious, and would not wake up, but she was alive. Had a large knot on the back of the head. Looks like she may have fallen from one of them trees. Well, the soldiers didn't want nothing to do, so we took her."

"They didn't want her you say?" the captain asks.

"No. They said it was fine for us to take her, since they already had a whole bunch locked up. They also mentioned a long trip they was taking to move a whole lot of 'em, didn't want no more of 'em," Peter says.

The captain pulls away from the table, looks out the front cabin window, into the night and says, "She must have been following us, must have been part of that tribe we picked up."

"What? Oh, ok. Uh, like I was sayin', I need a good scout—someone that can find the young black negro and hold her fo' me till I return this way," says Peter.

The captain turns to Peter, leans toward him and asks, "And what about the Indian girl?"

"Really don't care about her… Do whatever you want w' her," Peter says.

The captain flashes a wide smile as he stands up. He looks over at Peter and picks up a small piece of meat from his plate. "I'm assuming there is payment for such services to be rendered?"

Peter returns the grin and nods. "Well, o' course. My employer would not have it any othe' way."

The captain walks over to the window and looks outside. The camp is very still. A soft breeze moves the top of the trees slightly from side to side. He sees the soldiers changing guard by the gate. The light of the moon floods the whole area. "The caravan has already left, taking the bulk of the soldiers in this fort with it."

He turns around and walks back to Peter, who looks at the captain from his spot at the table with expectation.

The lamp shining on one side of his face lights up his crooked smile.

Captain Francis stands in front of Peter, not saying anything.

Peter feels a bit uncomfortable, with a mammoth of a man looking down on him, and says, "Well, there would be a sizable sum going to you personally…at least for all yo' trouble, of course."

The captain looks at the fireplace, then at Peter from the side of his eye and says, "Of course. Well I do believe you're in luck sir." He takes a few steps back, turns around, and looks at Peter with a smile. "I know a really good Indian tracker. I've seen him work myself, and he's good— and fast!"

"There we go!" exclaims Peter, his southern drawl continuing.

"I'm not due to leave here for two and a half months. I don't have men to spare, but I do believe that I can help you myself!"

Peter slams his hand down on the table with excitement, and yells, "Alright now!"

The captain stops smiling, and a serious look takes over his face. He looks at Peter for a few seconds and asks, "How much?"

Peter smiles and says, "The usual goin' rate to find a slave is twenty dollars—that's what we pay our boys. But since this is a special favor to us on your behalf, I'll go ahead and make it thirty-five fo' you."

The captain smirks and sits back down on his stool. He looks at Peter with a wry grin and says, "You're going to give me three hundred dollars, that nice big gold ring you're wearing, and a sincere and heartfelt thank you."

Peter is flabbergasted by the proposal and looks around the room as if there was someone else as a witness to this. "What?" asks Peter.

"That's my fee. I'll get that girl by the end of the week," says the captain.

Peter slaps his knee. "Now that's absurd!"

Before Peter could blink, the captain picks up a large hunting knife from the table, grabs Peter by his shirt, and puts the knife at his throat. Slowly, the captain puts his face right in front of Peter's. "I don't think you understands the situation you are in right now."

Peter squirms in his seat as the captain slowly pushes the knife against soft flesh.

"Captain, have you lost yo' mind?" whispers Peter.

"I know you slavers have money, and if you don't pay me what I'm worth… Well then, I'll kill you right here—right now," says the captain.

"What?" asks Peter.

The captain smiles, a mad glare upon his face. "That's right. I'll tell them you came into my quarters unannounced, complaining about your lost slaves, demanding that something be done. I asked you to leave,

you refused and attacked me, push came to shove and…
Oops, I had to defend myself from a crazy man.”

Peter shakes his head. He can’t believe it. “No, I
would neva’. No!” he yells.

The captain easily picks Peter off his feet with one
hand. Like a rag doll, he walks him over to the opposing
wall and slams him against it. His large stature
overshadows Peter’s frame. “I’ll even have an eyewitness,”
says Captain Francis.

“Please. Please!” Peter begs, crying as the captain
brings the knife up to his eyeball.

“The pretty little boy you saw earlier? He will say
anything just to keep Daddy happy. He was coming to
deliver my shinned boots, and saw you attack me, you
see…”

“Lies… These ah just made-up stories.”

The captain brings the knife closer to Peter's eye, draws in closer and says, "It won't matter. You'll be dead… Now pay up!"

Peter slowly reaches into his pocket and pulls out a bundle of money.

The captain immediately drops him and says, "I knew you had money!"

As Peter begins to count out the money, the captain snatches it all from his hand, leaving the man distraught. The captain quickly counts the money and shoves it in his pocket.

"That's a lot mo' than three hundred…" Peter dares to argue.

The captain holds out his hand to Peter and says, "And the ring!"

"W…what?' asks Peter. He looks down at the large gold ring on his right hand and says, "Th…this was a gift."

The captain puts the knife back on the slaver's throat and looks at him grimly. Peter slowly and reluctantly pulls the ring off his hand and holds it out to the captain.

Captain Francis snatches it, smiles wide and says, "Well…that was good business, sir. I know you must be going."

Peter looks at the captain, in complete disbelief of what just happened. He rubs his neck and, despite everything that has transpired, ventures to ask one more thing. "So, we have an understanding then?"

The captain walks over to the front door, opens it wide and gestures for Peter to exit. He looks at Peter and says, "By the end of the week, that young negro will be my prisoner, she will be held in this encampment until your return."

Peter walks over to the door, but he stops at the threshold. "And the Indian girl?"

"Our arrangement was for the black slave, unless you want to negotiate for her capture as well?"

"No, I was just curious," says Peter.

"In that case, and to satisfy your curiosity, I will probably fuck that Indian dead. Now get out!"

Peter exits the cabin, and in the moment he turns around to regard the captain one last time, he notices an air of superiority on the big man's face.

"Well?" Asks the captain.

"Uh…what?" asks Peter.

"You should be thanking me," says the captain.

Peter sends a look of confusion the captain's way. But all it takes is a subtle raising of Captain Francis's eyebrows for him to pipe up. "Thank you captain?"

"It's got to be heartfelt…sincere-like, or it doesn't count," says Captain Francis as he twirls the knife in his hand.

Peter straightens himself up, and says, "Captain, from the bottom of my heart, I sincerely thank you for your services."

"You're welcome," says the captain, before slamming the door in his face.

Peter slowly turns around and defeatedly walks away from the captain's cabin. He looks back at the cabin, then looks up at the sky and says, "Would've been better off looking for them myself…"

Chapter 3: The Tough Roads Ahead

It is a partly sunny day. Warm rays shine brightly through the clouds, forcibly appearing and disappearing as the large white cumulus clouds shift. The mass of natives and soldiers travel slowly through the trail in the wilderness below. Cries, weeping and moaning mixes in with the sound of horses and wagons moving. A cloud of dust and dirt rises.

Isi slowly opens her eyes and sees an old, wrinkled native woman weeping across from her. Isi sits up and sees that she's on the back of a covered wagon filled with supplies. She is surrounded by barrels, packages, boxes and trunks of all different types, crates of jars filled with preserved food, and bags of grain. She looks over at the woman again and realizes that there is a dead body wrapped in a blanket right beside her on the floor. The old woman looks at her and continues to cry softly as she gently pats the body.

"Where am I? Whose wagon is this?" asks Isi.

"I think she's awake," says a voice from the front of the wagon.

Isi looks in the direction the voice came from and sees Jean and a young native man sitting outside the canopy, at the front of the wagon. Jean crouches down, looks back at Isi and smiles.

"Good morning. Hi. Well, you're in *my* wagon. You were sleeping so soundly this morning, I had Biisan here pick you up and put you in our wagon," says Jean, as Isi looks at him shocked, with her mouth open. "Better that than have one of those soldiers beat you awake with the butt of their rifle," Jean says.

"What?" asks Isi.

"I didn't think you'd mind. It's better than walking at least, right?" asks Jean. He points to the young man next to him and says, "This is Biisan. He's a good friend. He's been working with me for a few years now…"

Biisan crouches down, pops his head in and greets Isi. "Hello."

Isi does not answer. She looks over at the body on the floor and asks, "Is…is this a dead body?"

Jean gives the reins to Biisan and tries to make his way to the back of the wagon. The road is uneven and bumpy, leaving the wagon jostling every few feet. Jean almost loses his footing as he makes his way to the back. Isi stares at him as he goes and sits beside the old woman. He places his arm around her shoulders and says, "It's her husband. He died sometime in the night."

Isi points to the old lady's feet. They are mangled and wrapped in bloody bandages. "Her feet are bleeding," Isi says.

Jean looks down at her feet, then back at Isi and says, "One of the reasons why she's here. Also, she's on her own, and she was not going to be able to bury or carry her husband. We're going to help her, and bury her husband tonight when we stop."

The old woman covers her face with her hands and begins to cry louder now. Jean brings the old lady closer to him as he hugs her and begins to pat her on the shoulder. The woman buries her face in his chest and continues to weep.

Isi stares at them. Her eyes begin to water as a flood of emotions begin to hit her in the chest: the loss of her mother and younger brother, not knowing where her sister is, and where she is going to end up… It hits her all at once.

She turns and looks out the back of the wagon to the dusty road, the walking natives, and the soldiers on horseback slowly making their march.

As she watches the scene unfold, she moves to the back of the wagon to get a better view. There are hundreds upon hundreds of natives walking—many families with little ones. There are a lot of old people, and just a few of them have horses, with even less having wagons. Some of them are hardly prepared for any type of travel of this sort. Many are barefoot and carry few provisions, if any.

A mother walking close to the wagon holds her baby at her breast as she walks, and a toddler follows her close as he holds on to her skirt, tears rolling down their eyes as they walk.

Isi makes eye contact with the woman and extends her arms toward her. "I can hold your baby for a while," Isi says.

The woman looks up at Isi and nods. She hands her the baby, and Isi takes the crying child into the wagon before sitting back down.

Jean, looking at everything from the front of the wagon, quickly gets up and makes his way to the back. Stepping over provisions, he quickly opens the rear door of the wagon and says, "Come on, sit up here with us."

The woman hands Jean the toddler. He takes the child and sits him beside Isi. He reaches out his hand and helps the young mother up onto the wagon.

"Thank you. Thank you so much," says the mother.

Jean pats the mother on her shoulder, then goes back and sits next to the elder. Isi watches closely as Jean reaches into one of the bags of sackcloth. She sees kindness in his eyes.

"You're not a soldier…" says Isi.

Jean pulls out an apple, and hands it to the toddler. The boy stops crying immediately and quickly bites into the apple.

"He was hungry," says Jean.

He hands one to the mother, who takes it gracefully. The old woman shakes her head when he offers her one, then he gives one to Isi and says, "No, I'm not a soldier. I'm a businessman. Originally from France. I came to this land years ago because of opportunity, just like everyone else."

Isi takes a bite of her apple and says, "To take advantage, just like everyone else."

This does not sit well with Jean, who understands where Isi is coming from, and feels the need to explain further. He adjusts his sitting position, and says, "No. I have traded thousands of pelts and goods over the years with the natives of this land. And have dealt fairly with you—as much as I was allowed anyway. Unlike the English, we've never had this type of ill will toward your people. The French have always gotten along with the natives I think. There was profit to be made on both sides, after all."

Jean holds out his arms and says, "But I fear that things have changed and will never go back to what we've known."

Isi's eyes swell with tears. She looks down at the dead body, then looks out through the back of the wagon and says, "Why are you helping me?" Isi wipes her eyes, looks down at the apple, and takes another bite.

Jean crosses his legs and says, "I'm on my way up north. I purchased some land, and I am planning on building a house. Maybe I'll even build the trading post. There's less risk in making a long journey in a group then doing it on my own, and that's why I am here. There's safety in numbers."

Isi looks down at the child sitting beside the old woman. He continues to eat the apple. The child looks up at her and holds it up for her to take a bite. Isi slightly smiles and pushes the apple back to his mouth. He jumps into Isi's arms and hugs her. She returns the embrace and gives him a kiss on the head. Isi then cradles him in her arms and begins to rock back and forth.

Jean smiles, but then puts on a stoic, reassuring face. "To answer your question, I'm helping you and whoever I can here. Because, though I cannot make up for the pain you have gone through and what you're going through, I can at least ease the burden a bit, as your people did for me when I first got here."

Isi looks at the young native man driving the wagon.

John turns and looks at him as well and says, "Biisan…his father and my father used to trade for years. I grew up in the business, and traveled with my father regularly. That's how we got acquainted. He was always curious about our way, our religion and things of that sort.

After his father died, Biisan wanted to come and work with me. He wanted to see France, and the white man's world, and he saw it, and like me, he grew tired of it quickly. We decided to stay. Just as he was of a great help to his father, he has been a help to me, so I could not refuse to come here, and start anew."

Jean looks at Isi and the child now asleep in her arms, still holding onto what's left of the apple. He takes the child from Isi's arms and sits back down, rocking the child back and forth. Jean asks, "Feel like sharing something about yourself?"

Isi looks away, and stares at the natives walking outside. "Why would a white man care about someone like me?" The apple falls from the child's hand, and Isi turns to look at Jean. He is looking down at the child in a pleasant way, enjoying what he is doing. Isi fixes her posture, and sits up straight and says, "I come from a proud people; my ancestors have lived on this land for a very long time, before my grandparents could remember. My family lived by the river for most of my life. We fished and hunted this land just like all our ancestors before us. We tried to get along with the whites, we tried to make trade, to coexist.

But they never wanted that, not really, regardless of the many lies they told us. In the end all they wanted was our land, and for us to disappear.

"Even after we agreed to leave, our chiefs signed on the paper and were given reassurance… It was a lie. Yesterday, soldiers attacked our camp and killed so many of us…"

Isi wipes tears as they fall from her eyes, her voice cracks as she continues, "My mother's head was opened… My baby brother, burned alive… That is all I can tell you about myself. I have become a shadow of pain, a wind of grief that will soon drift away."

"I'm so sorry…" says Jean.

Isi begins to weep, puts her head down and says, "We are leaving, but my grandfather's bones, and his grandfather's bones, remain behind. What will happen to us? I feel lost, I am lost…"

Isi picks her head up, wipes her tears, and looks at Jean. Her face is covered in pain. More tears begin to fall, and she says, "I was supposed to meet my sister Tula. I saw her at the soldier camp a few days ago. She said she would come, she said she would join me, but she never showed…"

Jean is filled with pity and concern for Isi. Hearing such a painful account strikes right at his heart. His eyes begin to swell with tears, and he says, "I am so sorry about your family, your people… There is nothing I can say that can mend what has been done, and my heart breaks for you. Isi, I do have some connections. I know someone important traveling with us. Let me see what I can find tonight about your sister. Please, allow me to help you."

Isi nods in approval. The old lady hands her a piece of cloth to dry her eyes. Isi takes it, but she is so deep in thought that she just holds it, as tears continue to fall from her eyes.

*   *   *

The day turns into night on the trail, and the sky is clear, filled with stars, with part of the Milky Way seen protruding from the top of the forest canopy. Plumes of smoke ascend into the sky from the campfires below. The travelers have set up camp, and some begin to settle in for the night.

A few tents are set up sporadically amongst the people. Some are tending to the sick and to the wounded. The road has already been strenuous on some. Many just sit by the fires idle, stoically looking as if searching for something that escapes them. Armed soldiers walk throughout the camp, looking on. They take shifts in guarding the perimeter. On the edges of the camp people bury their dead as they prepare for the following day. The sound of moaning and crying from old and young alike becomes a constant, common thing.

Jean and Biisan draw close to the tree line. Isi, the old lady, and the woman with the two children sit in front of a fire near the wagon not so far away. They all look at the men as they pack the dirt on the grave mound. The old woman shakes her head, her countenance filled with pain, the wrinkles on her face as if they have been formed by the tears that have fallen throughout the years, creating a perfect path for the new tears that are now falling onto her dress.

"This is not our way… This is not our way…" says the old lady.

Jean turns around, looks at the old lady and says, "I'm sorry, I know… But it's the best we can do for him now."

Isi stands up, walks over to the fire and adds another log. She stands and looks at Jean with a look of expectation.

Jean understands, quickly gives the shovel to Biisan and says, "Please keep watch until I return."

Biisan nods, and Jean walks out of their camp. Jean is heading to where the soldiers are staying.

He passes campfire after campfire as he heads to the back of the migration. Each group of people seems to be worse off than the last. Barefoot children and adults alike, people wounded, crying; many of them sit in silence. The feeling of loss is in the air. Heartbreak, despair and resentment are clearly visible on every face as he passes.

Many have lost the will to live, and now go through the motions of living.

John approaches a circle of wagons at the end of the migration encampment. The wagons are surrounded by guards. Laughter and loud talking can be heard coming out from within the camp. There are a few fires lit around the perimeter of the soldier encampment with a few soldiers sitting, and others going from fire to fire, talking and eating. Jean approaches one of the guards standing at the entrance of the soldier encampment.

"And where do you think you're going?" asks the guard.

Jean brushes off his jacket and says, "Oh, yes. Just need a word with the major."

The guard looks at Jean up and down and says, "What's your name mister?"

"Jean. Jean Lavigne. The major knows me. We've met before," says Jean.

The guard looks over to a young soldier standing by one of the wagons who was watching the whole exchange. He motions for him to come near. As the young soldier approaches, the guard says, "Take this man in and escort him to the major."

The soldier nods and leads Jean through the circle of wagons and into the camp. As the two walk into the camp, Jean is surprised to see what he finds within the large circle of wagons. There are many tents set up, and many fires, with soldiers merrily drinking and eating as if there was nothing wrong in the world. A soldier plays the harmonica while a few others dance to the music. Others clap their hands and smile as they watch. Soldiers laugh, eat and jesting. There seems to be plenty of food and drink to go around. The atmosphere is cheerful, completely different from everything that is going on outside. The major sits by a large fire with a few other military officers, eating and talking. As Jean and the soldier approach, the officers stop eating and put the plates down on their lap, looking at Jean with expectation.

The major recognizes Jean, smiles and says, "Mr. Lavigne…"

Jean stands before the major across from the fire, taken aback by the whole scene. He looks at the full plates of food, the drinks in their hands and the music playing. A soldier walks up to the major with a pitcher of what looks to be wine. The major and some of the other officers hold up their cups, and the soldier fills them one by one.

"Thank you soldier," says the major. The major takes a sip from his cup, looks over at Jean and asks, "So, Mr. Lavigne, is this journey everything you hoped it would be, sir?"

Everyone breaks out in laughter. The major himself cannot help but laugh a bit but tries to quickly compose himself.

"No. No, Major. There are food shortages already throughout. People are suffering. People are dying, sir," says Jean.

The major wipes his mouth and looks around at the officers around him as they smile at each other. "People?

People you say? I've heard no report of any man dying on my watch…" says the major.

"The natives, sir. I just helped bury one of the elders, not a few minutes before I came," replies Jean.

"Oh, you talk about these fucking Indians!" says the major.

Immediately, all the officers burst into fits of laughter.

"Sir, they need help. They—" Jean begins to speak.

"No! No sir, they are not people. These are savages, animals just like the beasts that roam these forests. They should be thankful for our protection!" says the major.

"Yeah!" all the officers and nearby soldiers cheer.

The Major continues to speak. "Without us, they would not make it through this wilderness at all!"

"Yeah!" the soldiers cheer again.

Jean can't believe what he is seeing.

The major takes another sip from his cup, takes out a handkerchief from his vest, and wipes his mouth. "We are just an escort Mr. Lavigne, nothing more. We are here to make sure the herd gets to where they're supposed to go, and then we go our merry way." The major holds his cup up to the officers, who join him and raise their cups as well. They all drink and laugh. The major takes a bite from a chicken drumstick and turns back to Jean. "So why have you come to see me Mr. Lavigne?"

Jean stands up straight and says, "Thank you, sir. Yes, I was talking to a young lady who was being housed in the fort you are stationed in. She says she lost her younger sister and—"

The Major quickly interrupts him. "Are you kidding me? You've come here for a lost sheep?"

Everyone breaks out in laughter again. Jean tries to keep himself composed, knowing that anything he says will be scrutinized, and things could go sideways quickly.

"Well yes sir, but—" Jean tries to say again before he is interrupted by the major.

"I cannot help you in this matter, Mr. Lavigne."

Jean interlaces his fingers before the commanding officer. "Please sir, if I could ask some of the soldiers, she said she saw her sister outside the fort a few nights ago, and now she's missing."

The major takes another bite from the chicken leg and does not answer.

Jean looks around at all the soldiers and says, "I'm glad for you. You have plenty of food and drink." Jean watches a nearby soldier get up, and throw food scraps into the fire. He is shocked and whispers to himself, "Those scraps could have fed someone."

The major throws the chicken bone onto his plate and says, "Mr. Lavigne, all I am concerned with is taking these animals to their destination as fast as possible. That's it. I know they are dying, and don't have sufficient food, and they are not equipped for this journey. But that is not our concern. They had time to prepare. They were warned. They should have been ready." The major looks at the soldiers around him and says, "Like we are…"

The officers around the fire nod in approval. Some raise their cups to him.

Jean looks at the major in dismay, and with disappointment.

"Anything else?" asks the major.

Jean, defeated, looks up at the major and says, "No. Thank you for your time, Major."

Jean turns around and walks away with his escort.

The major watches as Jean is led out, then suddenly he taps his forehead, reaches out to Jean and yells, "Mr. Lavigne!"

Jean turns around and quickly makes his way back to the major, who says, "I just remembered… Word did get to me after we departed that a young Indian girl was found near the southern perimeter of the fort during the night. It was a few days ago."

Jean's eyes widen with anticipation. He asks, "Where is the girl now?"

"Well, I don't know. She was picked up by members of a slave transport heading south. That is all I was told."

Jean's mouth drops.

*   *   *

The next day at a small clearing by the water's edge of the old slaver camp, Captain Francis and Abit, a native man, come out of the tree line on horseback. It is high noon, with not a cloud in sight. The air is thick with humidity, and everything is still, save for the calls of the birds in the trees. Captain Francis is out of uniform and dressed in common clothes a bit fancy for the wilderness, especially the freshly shined boots. Abit, an older middle-aged man with long braids, dressed in a poor white man's shirt and trousers, is focused on the ground below.

Abit gets off his horse, and the captain stops as well, watching every move that Abit makes intently. Abit softly walks toward the center of the camp with his hands open as if to feel the energy that was present. He reaches the center where there was burnt cinders and blackened logs present.

"There was a campfire here…"

The captain, from his horse, looks at the ash on the ground, and the remains of the burnt wood and says, "Really? How can you tell?"

Abit looks at the captain and stares at him for a few seconds.

The captain responds by raising his eyebrows and shrugging his shoulders and says, "Good job?"

Abit looks down again and slowly walks over to the water, following a trail. He looks past the captain and points. "There was a large wagon here. Then it went in your direction, a bit lighter than it arrived," Abit says. He turns around and walks toward the trees, kneeling to look closely at the area. "This is where the horses stayed."

Abit then looks a few feet away, and quickly walks into the forest. The captain climbs off his horse as fast as he can and follows Abit into the woods. Abit walks through bushes, over tall grasses, and in between trees. He walks until he breaks through a tree line and slowly moves toward the center of a small clearing. The captain walks after him but stays behind and observes.

Abit looks closely at the ground, walking slowly in a circle. He comes to a stop, kneels once more, and says, "Two youths were here… There was a third—a larger person."

The captain grows exited, and says, "Okay. Okay."

The native stands up and walk closer to a large tree and says, "Death… Someone died here. It was the large one. This is where he fell."

The captain slaps his hands together and says, "This is it. This is where that slaver died, it has to be! Where did they go Abit?"

Abit walks up to the captain, looking at the ground. He's following something. He stops right beside the captain, looks at him and says, "The two left on a horse. The tracks came from the camp, and lead in the opposite direction."

The captain smiles, and spits tobacco on the ground. "This is why I love you, Abit!"

Abit ignores him and walks into the woods, the captain on his heels. They walk back to the slaver camp, following the horse tracks. Abit comes out of the tree line and walks right into the slaver camp toward the trees where the horses were previously held. He stops looks at the ground and says, "All the horses follow the wagon, except for the tracks leading to the other clearing. Those are the tracks we must follow. The girls are on that horse."

The captain slaps his hands together and says, "Hot damn. This is why I love you Abit. I ever tell you that?"

"Yes, about a minute ago," says Abit.

Suddenly, a very large owl flies down from the sky and hits the captain. The bird smacks him on the face so hard that it makes a loud sound. The captain bends down and tries to swat at the bird, but the owl quickly flies away unharmed. The captain, on the other hand, has a large cut on his left cheek, right under his eye. Blood quickly begins to flow from his wound. He takes a handkerchief out of his pocket and holds it against the scratch. He turns to look at Abit, who is staring back at him as if he's seen a ghost.

"What?" shouts the captain.

Abit stares at the captain without saying a word for some time. Then he finally says,
"Bad omen… Death."

The captain shakes his head. He grows angry and spits on the ground as he looks at Abit. "No. No, no…no! It's not a bad omen, just a stupid bird. C'mon. Let's go get those girls!"

The captain walks toward his horse in anger, and climbs on as he holds onto his face, the handkerchief now covered in blood.

Abit continues to stand there, frozen by fear. He looks up at the trees and sees the owl looking down at him. Abit shakes his head and says, "This is a bad omen."

Chapter 4: Friendships and Hardships

The light of the sun scarcely makes its way through the tree canopy above. Within the woods, in a very secluded place where birds, deer and all types of forest creatures rest, lies the small mouth of a cave. The mouth of the cave is covered by vines, grasses and vegetation, and it is barely visible with its camouflage. A deer feeding nearby lifts its head and quickly runs into the woods. Birds and rabbits take off as Tula and Abeke break through the tree line. The horse stops short, right in front of the cave opening. The girls look around the small clearing and see the last of the birds fly away, and suddenly, everything is still again.

The girls can't help but stare at the cave opening as rays of light pierce through the branches, lighting a path into it. Tula gets off her horse and slowly walks to the opening. As she does, she looks around for movement in the forest. She pushes some of the ivy to the side, and peers inside, then looks back at Abeke and smiles.

"I know this place," she says.

Tula walks back to the horse and helps Abeke get oof the horse. Abeke rubs her pregnant belly and nods a thank you.

"So you've been here…" says Abeke.

Tula walks back to the entrance, and puts her hand on the rock wall as if touching something familiar. She glides her hand across the rocks, smiles, looks back at Abeke and walks in. "Bring the horse," says Tula.

Abeke shakes her head and whispers to herself, "But why?"

Tula disappears through the small entrance of the cave. Abeke looks around and sees nothing but trees, and reluctantly follows, pulling the horse with her.

After they pass the small entrance, Abeke sees that the cavern inside is expansive. They walk on dirt and gravel down the very long and dimly lit gray rocky passageway. Natural light comes from what looks like an entrance into a room at the end of the corridor and illuminates the way. The girls enter a vast open room within the cave. Inside, the walls are solid gray rock. Fine dirt covers the ground, and it looks like somebody has been here before.

There are piles of wood and sticks gathered in one area, and piles of stone in another. In the middle, there are the remains of an old campfire, encircled by stones. Right above the circle of stones, on the roof of the cave, there is a large hole in the center of the ceiling where the light of the sun shines through. Vegetation, a mix of vines and roots, creeps in through the aperture in the ceiling. Tula slowly approaches the center of the fire pit and looks around. She hears the noise behind her and quickly turns. It is Abeke entering the room with the horse in tow.

"My father brought me and my cousins here before," Tula says. She walks around the remains of the campfire as she looks around the cave, and then she walks toward the pile of sticks, picks one up and says, "Father taught me how to hunt, how to fish. Here he would tell us stories." Tula looks down the length of the stick, checking to see how straight it is. "I learned a lot from my father. Last time we were here we gathered these materials to make bows, and arrows. It was night. We were going on the hunt the next day."

Abeke looks at Tula as she hears her story. She holds her pregnant belly and sits on one of the rocks close to the fire pit. Tula looks around the pile and finds what looks like twine. She begins to tie it to one of the ends of the stick she found. She is making a bow.

"One of my cousins was feeding the fire and had brought in a large pile of wood," Tula explains. She leans into the piece of wood, bending it as she puts her weight into it. Then she ties the other end, completing her construction. "Father went to the pile of wood and when he reached to get one, a viper hidden within the pile bit my father's arm. We tried to get it off him, but we could not, even though we pulled and pulled. Finally, I grabbed a burning log from the fire and as I pressed it against the snake it finally let go. But it was too late, the viper had injected of much of its poison into my father. He fell ill almost immediately. He went to sleep a few hours later, and never woke up. He went to be with our ancestors."

Tula holds the bow out in front of her, and displays it to Abeke, who watches her carefully.

"What he taught me continues to live in me today. And for that, I am grateful," Tula says.

Abeke spots a sharp hand tool by the old campfire. Tula sees it and extends her hand to her. Abeke places it in her hand. Tula walks over to the large pile of sticks, picks one up, and begins to sharpen one of the ends, crafting a crude arrow.

Abeke sees her and nods her head in approval. She says, "I never knew my father. An elder of your people, the Choctaw, they bought my mother from a white man when she was very young, and pregnant with me. Chochopi was his name."

Tula comes and sits beside Abeke on a nearby stone.

Abeke continues to speak. "I will tell you the story of my beginnings. Imagine a beautiful bright day, warm in the spring. A large cabin stands by a meadow amongst tall willow trees. There is grass all around the cabin, and birds sing their songs. A native man, his wife and his two sons live in this cabin. The cabin has a porch, and the family has horses. There's a beautiful garden close to the house where vegetables grow. My mother would tend to it amongst all the other chores that she was responsible for.

I was born on this farm, and as I grew up, I helped my mother with all the chores, like cleaning, washing, cutting wood, tending to the horses, and even making meals. I learned to speak with my mother in her native tongue, but I learned Choctaw from Chochopi's family. His oldest son and I would often go off and play together, chasing each other around the garden, and hiding behind the trees nearby. He took a liking to me from a very young age. We would spend every day together in one way or another.

Things were different when we were in front of his parents. My mother and I would sit in another section of the cabin while they ate. We were allowed to eat after they were done. The cabin was quaint, decorated with American Indian tapestries and artwork. For the most part everything was fine for many years. I learned my place and at least I had a roof over my head.

We were close friends, the boy and I. And as we grew up, we started liking each other in a different way. We would sneak off at night and head into the woods. We would run over the small hill nearby and go to the riverside. It was there that he would enter me. Sometimes we would go into the water and play afterwards. Sometimes we would rest in one another's arms. And he promised me that he would be my man."

Tula puts an arrow down, walks over to the pile, grabs a few more sticks and says, "It doesn't sound like you had it that bad. How did you end up as a slave?"

Abeke looks at Tula with pain and resentment, and says, "As Chochopi's son got a bit older, his appetite for me grew. He was not just taking me in the night, but on every occasion that he could get his hands on me. I didn't refuse him, I loved him, and I believed he loved me. He was on top of me every day, and everything was flowers, until my belly began to show. I didn't care, I wanted to have his child. I really did love him, but his mother began to hate me.

"One day she came into the barn when I was brushing off one of the horses. The door swung open, and she burst in, came directly at me, and hit me in the face. I fell to the ground, and she continued to hit me. When I tried to shield myself from her, she bit my hand. Chochopi ran into the barn and pulled his wife off me, but she continued to scream at him, hitting him on the shoulder. With anger she pointed at me, and I could feel the hatred in her when she told me she wanted me to go.

"From that day on she continued to beat me on an almost daily basis. She pressed her husband to get rid of me. Day after day she nagged him, and she did not let up. He didn't want to do it—he said there was value in me having a child, that it was also his blood—*their* blood—but she did not care. She began to make everyone's life a misery, after a few months he finally gave in.

"I'll never forget that day. Chochopi and his wife were standing at the door of their cabin as a slaver wagon pulled up with men and horseback accompanying the wagon. The men got off their horses and waited. The driver of the wagon nodded at Chochopi, and he pointed to me while I was standing in the garden, close to the house. Without a word being spoken, the horsemen walked up to me and grabbed me by the arms and by the neck. They put chains on me. My mother tried to pull me away, but she could not. She begged Chochopi, but his mind was already made-up.

"My mother asked the men to take her instead, but they just pushed her away and down to the ground. They were too strong for her. They put me in the back of that metal wagon and took me away. I grabbed the bars and looked at my mother as she cried on her knees and reached out to me, tears falling down her face as she grabbed her heart. I was crying as well. I couldn't help it. It was the worst day of my life. I can still hear her screams…

"But I still have this baby inside me. I know who the father is, and I can tell the child that they was born out of love… At least I can tell them that."

Tula puts another arrow down and asks, "What was his name? The boy."

Abeke looks down at her pregnant belly, rubs it and says, "It don't matter, not worth sayin' anyways."

Abeke turns to look at Tula with tears in her eyes and sees that she has stopped working on the arrows. She's looking up at something in the hole of the caves ceiling. Abeke looks up and cannot see anything. She stands up to get a better look, but Tula motions for her to stop moving.

"Shh…" says Tula.

Abeke looks up again to the large hole in the ceiling and behind some bushes up there, close to the edge, she sees it; a hulking mountain lion looks right down at Tula. The lion is motionless and stoic. Tula slowly rises as she holds the bow and arrow, but she does not point it. She observes cautiously. The lion slowly gets up from his crouched position, looks at Abeke, then looks back at Tula and yawns. It licks its paw then slowly walks away.

"We should leave," whispers Abeke.

"No, it's not hunting us," Tula says. "It would not have revealed itself the way it did. No, we will be safe here. We should rest for a while, then move on."

"How can you tell?" Abeke asks.

Tula and Abeke look at each other for a few seconds without saying a word, then Tula says, "The lion spirit within him told me so…"

Again, there are a few seconds of silence as they stare into each other's eyes. Then Abeke says,
"We should build a fire; I will gather some wood."

"One of those rabbits out there will make a good meal and give me a chance to test my bow," Tula says. "We should get some grass for the horse."

Abeke smiles and nods in approval. Tula continues to make arrows as Abeke begins to gather pieces of wood scattered throughout the cave.

*   *   *

The sun quickly sets. Birds fly above the treetops of the forest as they sing and prepare for the night to come. The last few rays of sunlight quickly disappear behind the tree line. Tula and Abeke, after a few hours of rest, come out of the forest, riding their horse and make their way to the east shoreline of the Mississippi River nearby. They stop short and stare with their mouths open as they see a large Steamboat filled with hundreds of native people. The boat is so close to their side of the river that they can see the whites of the eyes of the people onboard. Native men, women and children, packed like sardines are on every level of the boat, with no standing room left. No one is talking on the boat, or hardly moving for that matter. There is an eerie, somber silence that rests on the vessel.

Suddenly, from the very top level of the boat, two white men walk up to the railing, and quickly throw a dead native man's body overboard. The body crashes into the water, then resurfaces beside the boat as the current takes it away. The girls look at the body and follow it with their eyes as it travels past them and continues downstream.

Suddenly a baby cries out within the boat somewhere. The girls quickly look back in that direction, but they cannot see the baby, just hundreds of solemn eyes looking back at them in somber silence.

The girls stare at the boat as it passes them, and slowly travels upriver. They stay there, sitting on the horse, watching as it slowly disappears into the distance.

Tula and Abeke look at each other, then look at the river at the same time.

"We have to get across this river," Tula says.

"How? It's so wide. The horse will drown!" Abeke says.

"No, the horse can make it. Can you?" Tula asks.

"I can keep my head afloat if that's what you mean," says Abeke.

Tula begins to navigate the horse into the water slowly and says, "If the water gets strong, we need to try and stay together."

The horse carefully enters the water, and the girls begin to make their way across the river. The water slowly rises to the legs of the horse, then to its broad chest as they descend deeper into the river.

"This water is cold!" Abeke says.

"Steady, steady…" says Tula as they continue to press forth into the river.

The water reaches the neck of the horse. It swims and is beginning to drift down river. The girls hold on to the horse for dear life, their bodies submerged in the water.

The turbulent waters, and the pull of the river is so strong, that Abeke is pulled from the horse. Tula reaches for her with one hand, but is pulled away from the horse herself and goes under. The water is choppy, and the river moves fast. The horse, terrified, continues to swim by himself now as it tries to get to the other side. Abeke sees the horse a few feet away, and tries to swim toward it as she struggles to stay afloat. She looks for Tula, but she cannot find her in the water.

"Tula! Tula where are you?" Abeke screams.

A piece of driftwood finds its way to Abeke. She grabs it in a desperate hold and continues to look around for Tula. She arduously makes her way toward the other side of the river as she looks around in every direction, but Tula is nowhere to be found. Slowly Abeke moves through the rapids until she finally reaches the western riverbank.

"Tula!" Abeke yells as she comes out of the water holding her belly.

Abeke is exhausted. She crawls into shallow waters and struggles to get off of her belly and sit. Where is Tula, she thinks to herself, worried. But she is unable to move her cold body then. She takes a few deep breaths, gathers up whatever strength she has inside her, slowly turns around and stands by the riverbank, alone and wet. Troubled, she does not see her friend anywhere as she scans the river.

"Tula! Tula where are you?" Abeke yells.

But there is no answer.

Abeke takes the rag of a dress she has on off her wet body and wrings the water out of it a few times. She looks around. No Tula. She walks up the bank and beats the dress against a tree to get as much water out of it as possible.

"Tula! Tula!" Abeke yells again, as she puts her dress back on.

She begins to walk upriver, looking for Tula as she goes, her companion nowhere to be seen. As she slowly makes her way up the river, she looks on the opposite side as well. Maybe she never made it across, she thinks. The sun has completely set, and the last of the light of day is quickly fading. Abeke looks up at the sky, worried that she'll never see Tula again. She stops. All she can hear is the rushing of the river, but then suddenly, she hears movement. Something is approaching her position. She quickly runs and takes cover behind river grasses and reeds, and carefully watches the tree line. It's getting closer and closer, but it does not sound like something big.

Suddenly, Tula jumps out of the brush, her mouth and hands covered in what looks like black and blue ink.

"Berries!" she yells, and quickly runs back into the woods.

Abeke quickly gets up and follows her, yelling, "Tula, I've been looking for you. Wait! Where are you going?"

The girls run through the forest downriver, until they get to a small clearing. Tula finally reaches a whole bunch of blackberry bushes by the side of the riverbank and begins to pick the berries. She urges Abeke to join her as she motions for her to come. Abeke watches as Tula fills her mouth with so many berries, she can hardly chew.

"Whad a yu wading fo?" asks Tula with her mouth full.

Abeke runs to the bushes and begins to pick the berries as well, watching Tula as she fills her pockets with them. The girls then hear something in the bushes nearby and suddenly stop. They look at each other in fear. Before they can do anything, to their surprise, their horse comes out of the woods, slowly walks past them, and begins to chew on tender river grasses by the water. The girls look at each other again and laugh. As they laugh, a piece of a berry flies out of Tula's nose and hits Abeke on the forehead. The girls keel over with laughter.

Chapter 5: Pestilence and Death

The next morning, a world away, the barefoot steps of a young native girl can be heard slapping against trail beneath her. One blistered bloody foot drags in front of the other and slaps down, picking up dirt, step by step. Wagons pass her by, and horses, and they disturb the ground beneath her, kicking up a dust cloud that coats the young girl's face as they move, drawing a cough from deep within her lungs. People walking past her ignore her until finally she's overwhelmed with emotions, and she begins to weep. Exhausted, the girl falls to her knees, leans forward and throws up. Her eyes close as she faints, and falls face-first, into her own vomit.

People continue to walk past her, talking, some crying as they walk over her as if she did not exist. The large clouds above expose and hide the sun as they move across the sky. The rays of sunlight hit the girl's body then disappear, repeatedly, as if signaling for someone to help.

A middle-aged native woman sees the young girl on the ground and kneels beside her. She turns the girl over and puts her hand on her chest. She leans toward her and hears her breathing. The woman realizes that the young girl is still alive and quickly picks her up. She looks around for help, but no one seems to care. The migrants continue to move past her as she stands in the middle, looking for someone—anyone—who would be willing to help.

"Please, someone help! Can anyone help please?" the woman cries out.

But no one responds.

The woman sees two soldiers on horseback approaching her. She knows that she's not going to get any help from them, so she quickly turns around and ambles along with the rest of the migrants to blend in. As soon as the soldiers pass her, she turns around again to face everyone. She sees Jean Lavigne's wagon approaching. Jean holds the reins of the horses as Isi sits beside him. They both see the woman trying to hold up the little girl as Jean's wagon approaches.

"Please… Please…" the woman faintly says, her voice drowned by the moving of the crowd.

Isi spots the woman. She pats Jean on the shoulder repeatedly and points to her. Jean immediately turns the direction of the wagon to the woman. He slows the horses, gives the reins over to Isi, and jumps out to take the young girl from her arms. Jean runs to the back of the wagon, now finally stopped, and releases the lock, allowing the back door to fall. Isi helps the woman climb the front of the wagon and take a seat beside her.

Jean, puts his hands on the girl's forehead and says, "She's burning up!"

The woman that was holding the young girl says, "Medicine. She needs medicine!"

Jean climbs the wagon, and begins to root through his belongings. He moves bags and heavy containers around. He begins to hand things to Isi as he looks through a large crate.

"I don't have anything that will act quick enough to bring her fever down!" he says.

Isi looks at the people passing by and says, "Maybe we can ask. Maybe someone will have something that will help!"

Jean nods in agreement. Isi jumps off the wagon and begins to ask passers-by for fever medicine. One after the other, they shake their heads or tell her they don't have anything. In the meantime, Jean takes water from his canteen and soaks his handkerchief. He pours some water into the girl's mouth and presses the handkerchief against her forehead.

A soldier on horseback rides up and sees Jean in the back of the wagon, working on the woman as Isi pleads with people as they walk past her.

"What's all this?" the soldier asks.

Jean looks up at the soldier and responds, "This girl is very sick; we're trying to get her some medicine to bring this devilish fever down."

The soldier brings his horse closer to the back of the wagon and takes a look while Jean helps the girl, and Isi stops every passerby. "I see… Well, you need to get this wagon moving, mister. Got no time to stop for the sick."

Jean and the soldier lock eyes for a few seconds. Jean's disgust can clearly be seen on his face as he bites his lip. The soldier, on the other hand, welcomes this anger with a slight smile, as he gently puts his hand on his rifle.

Jean slowly nods in agreement. He knows better than to provoke this idiot soldier.

"Sorry, sir… We'll get the wagon moving straight away," Jean says.

The soldier takes a good look at the native girl in Jean's care. He sees that her face has been beaten by the sun, and that her bloody feet are covered with broken blisters. And in that moment, he feels pity in his heart. He looked over at Isi, standing by the wagon. She was looking back at him, and he could see her longing for him to have mercy on this girl.

"Tell you what Mr. Lavigne… Get one of these folks here to drive your wagon, so we can get it moving. You and I, we'll ride up the procession here and talk to Charlie. If anyone has anything to shake a fever, he will."

Jean smiles at the soldier, and motions for the old lady siting close to him to take the young girl into her arms. The old lady moves quickly past Biisan who sits beside her, kneels on the floor of the wagon and rests the woman's head on her lap.

Jean looks at them and says, "I will be right back. I'm going with the soldi to get medicine."

"Good. She doesn't have long," Biisan says.

Jean quickly moves to the back of the large wagon and climbs on the back of the soldier's horse. Isi looks at him, not knowing what is happening.

"Get the wagon moving, we're going to get medicine for the girl!" says Jean.

Before Isi can respond, the soldier kicks the horse and it takes off running, Jean barely holding on. They maneuver, and weave in and out of hundreds of natives, soldiers, and wagons on the trail. Jean looks forward as he tries to get a fix as to where the soldier is taking him. The large amount of dust is picked up by a breeze and carried up toward the sky.

As they approach a large wagon filled with supplies, Jean sees an old soldier holding onto the reins. He swats at the air, stands, then sits down and screams at himself as they approach. The soldier with Jean on his back slows the horse down to match the wagon's speed and gets right beside Charlie.

"I know, I know. But that's not the way it went! I'm telling you he's the one that did it!" screams Charlie.

Jean looks at Charlie with a little disdain as he sees he's a little off his rocker.

Charlie is startled by the men riding beside him, jumps and says, "What the hell!"

Jean tips his hat and says, "Sorry about that sir. Didn't mean to startle you there. My name is Jean, Jean Lavigne."

Charlie spits, and angrily looks at Jean and the soldier. He slowly moves back to his stool and sits down as he wipes his forehead. He continues to look at the men and they stare back. Charlie grabs a canteen from below his bench, takes a sip and looks back at the men.

"What? What you want?" yells Charlie.

"Charlie, you got anything for fever in your medical box?" asks the soldier.

Charlie looks straight ahead, as if the men were not there, and says, "Who said I had anything like that?"

The soldier takes his hat off and lightly hits Charlie on the shoulder. "C'mon Charlie. The man here can trade," says the soldier.

Charlie just looks at them without saying a word.

"I have some money. I'm willing to buy it," says Jean.

Jean pulls out a bill clip from his pocket and shows it to Charlie, but Charlie is unimpressed and spits on the ground.

"I don't want no money… What good is money out here anyway?" Charlie says.

"So, we can trade then…" Jean says.

Charlie gives him a slight nod and says, "Whatcha got?"

Jean reaches down his shirt and pulls out a large and intricate Native American necklace he's wearing. It's beautifully decorated with native stones and feathers.

Charlie looks at it for a few seconds and says, "Nope."

Jean looks down at the boots that Charlie wears, and notices that they are not military issued boots. Charlie wears expensive snakeskin cowboy boots.

Jean looks back in the direction of his wagon, looks back at Charlie and says, "Well, I've got some nice crocodile skin that I can give you in exchange for something to help the girl."

"Do you now… Well, that's something, I reckon. I can give you some syrup I got for the fever in exchange for that skin."

"There you go!" says the soldier.

"We'll be right back," says Jean with a smile, the soldier already turning the horse around.

*   *   *

A little way from them, Isi sits at the front of the wagon holding the reins, rocking as the wagon travels across the tough terrain. In the distance ahead of her, she sees dirt being kicked up in the air. It's coming her way, and she realizes that it's Jean and the soldier. Isi stands up and waves at them as they race toward her.

The men reach the rear of the wagon and see Biisan sitting on the edge, holding the child, and the old lady changing wet rags on the girl's forehead.

Jean, still on the horse, points to a bunch of bundles inside the wagon and says, "Someone quickly hand me the bottom package there! The one all the way at the bottom."

Biisan hands the child to the old lady, gets up and begins to move things around to retrieve package. He looks back at Jean and asks, "What are you doing?"

"I think that we may have found someone that has a syrup for her fever. I need the alligator skin to trade for it."

Biisan pulls out one of the packages and lifts it up to show Jean, asking, "How's this one?"

Jean holds out his hands and says, "That'll do!"

Biisan throws him the wrapped skin. Jean tucks it under his armpit and slaps the soldier's shoulder.

"Let's go!" says Jean.

The two ride up the trail again, leaving a cloud of dust in their wake as they move around groups of people, slowly making their way through the wilderness.

Charlie sits on his wagon, sipping from a flask of whisky. He holds it up to a native family as he passes them, and in mockery he says, "How do you do!"

When the boys ride up to him, bringing a cloud of dust with them, Charlie is startled once more. Dust gets into his mouth, and he tries to spit it out as he tries to close the lid to his flask.

"Stop doing that!" Charlie says.

Jean takes the alligator skin and tosses it at Charlie. Charlie musters to catch the skin but drops his whiskey flask on the floor of the wagon.

"Dog gone it! Look what you made me do!" he says.

Charlie struggles to keep the reins of the wagon, and the gator skin on his lap as he reaches down to get the flask, when he finally gets it, he accidentally drops it again, it bounces off his boot, and onto the ground below. Charlie looks back and sees one of the native men picks up the flask, opens it, drinks from it, and lifts it up to Charlie.

"Sonofabitch!" mutters Charlie.

"Come on Charlie, we don't have time to waste here!" says the soldier.

"All right, all right! Hold on a minute!" he shouts.

With the wagon still moving, Charlie puts the reins on the seat and disappears into the back of the wagon. He moves boxes around, and starts digging through crates, until he finally finds what he's looking for. He walks back to the front with it: a metal box with a red cross painted on it. He gets back to the front of the wagon, sits down, and puts the box on his lap. Jean and the soldier wait with anticipation, but know that it is taking too long.

Charlie opens the box and takes out a dark brown bottle. Jean reaches for it, but Charlie holds his index finger up to him. He reaches for the package Jean gave him. He opens it and says, "Indeed… It is an alligator skin, so here's your syrup."

Jean snatches the bottle from Charlie's hand and says, "Let's go!"

The soldier kicks his horse, yelling, "C'mon!"

The soldier races the horse against the flow of the migration, like a boat against the current. They ride back to Jean's wagon, navigating in and out as they avoid the people walking by. In the distance they see Isi and Biisan sitting on the front of the wagon, but they're not waving, not even moving. As they get close, Isi and Biisan don't say anything but somberly stare at them. Jean, fearing the worst, motions the soldier to head to the back of the wagon. The horse gets to the back and matches the speed of the wagon as Jean and the soldier look in. The girl is covered by a blanket, lying flat on the floor of the wagon, motionless. The old lady sitting beside her looks at Jean and shakes her head.

"The girl is dead. Her frail body completely gave out on her. It was too much," said the old woman.

The woman looks past Jean and the soldier and stares at the rest of the people walking, as a tear flows down her face.

Jean gets off the horse and begins to walk behind the wagon. He looks up at the soldier and says, "Thank you."

The soldier nods at Jean but does not speak. He takes a grim last look at the dead girl and rides off into the multitude of traveling souls.

Chapter 6: Going North

It's a partly cloudy day, and it's windy. The chirping of the birds is almost completely drowned out by the noise of the river flowing right beside Tula and Abeke. The girls are traveling north on the west side of the river, following a large dirt trail. They're tired and worn out. They've been on the move all day. Abeke plays with Tula's hair with one hand while she rubs her pregnant belly with the other.

"You know, you feel more and more like a sister to me," says Abeke.

Tula takes Abeke's hand, holds it to her heart and says, "That's good, because I am. I'm your sister now and there's nothing you can do about it."

"I'ma take care of you little sis… I always wanted to have a little sister, ha!"

Tula smiles before the horse enters what looks like a wall of willow tree branches. The girls fight to keep the branches from hitting them. Once they're through, they enter a large clearing.

Tula says, "Look at this"

They slowly approach a large group of natives resting by the riverbank, on a clearing underneath the canopy of towering willow trees. All of the natives stare at the girls as they approach from a distance on horseback. This group looks well supplied. They have many horses resting by the trees, and a lot of provisions. There are many families with children, a lot of young men, and some elderly people as well. They are relaxing as they eat in groups sitting by their campfires. As the girls approach, some of the men stand at attention and watch as the girls draw closer and closer.

Before entering their camp, Tula stops the horse and gets off.

Abeke stays on the horse, waves with her right hand, and smiles. "Hello," Abeke says in Choctaw.

An old native man gets up from amongst one of the groups sitting by a fire, he walks over to the girls without saying a word and without showing any expression on his face. The man has long white hair and wears necklaces and feathers over his brown shirt. His leather pants seem too big for him, and he struggles to keep them up as he walks. When he reaches the girls, he takes a long look at them both, and finally says, "They call me Talako. I am an elder of my tribe."

Tula smiles and says, "My name is Tula."

Abeke slowly unmounts the horse, stands next to Tula and says, "They call me Abeke."

Talako looks past the girls and into the woods behind them, then looks back at them and says, "You travel alone?"

"Yes," Abeke replies.

Talako is surprised by this claim and is immediately concerned about the girls.

"We travel north. My sister is with a large group heading to the new land. Hundreds of people—they have soldiers amongst them," says Tula.

Talako nods his head.

"Have you seen a large group traveling north?" asks Abeke.

The old man does not answer, but looks at the girls up and down, and then looks at their horse and says, "You are not equipped to make such a journey on your own. Join us. There is room."

Tula looks at Talako's people as they rest and sees many families with children playing around them. Young and old, they look like a tight community. She remembers her mother's smile, her laughter, and how she made her feel. Her heart longs to be with her people, but the longing to bring Isi and her new sister Abeke together wins her over.

"I need to find my sister," Tula says.

Talako looks at Tula and Abeke, concerned. He knows of the grave dangers out in this wilderness. He says, "It is safer to stay with us here for now. We will wait until tomorrow. More of my people will join us in the morning. We will all travel north together."

Abeke looks at Tula who is slightly shaking her head in disagreement.

"I don't think she wants to wait. If you could just point us in the direction that we should go… We don't want to be a burden."

The old man turns around and walks back to the group of people he is with. He says something to them softly and looks back at the girls as he does. A few of the women get up and pick up bags they are traveling with. They walk up to the girls without saying a word. One of them gives a large leather bag to Tula, and softly caresses her cheek. The other woman hands Abeke a large sackcloth bag, and reassures her by putting her hand on her shoulder. As the native women walk away, the girls look into the bags.

"This bag is filled with food," says Abeke, excited to see the provisions inside.

"This one has clothes in it," says Tula, just as happy.

As the women walk back to their camp, they cross paths with Talako, who is walking toward the girls with a horse. He walks up to Abeke, and hands her the reins. Abeke takes the reins, surprised at such a kind and generous gesture.

Talako says to her, "Take her. She is strong and fast. You will cover more ground this way."

Abeke jumps forward and hugs the old man. Talako is taken by surprise, startled by the sudden emotional response. As Abeke hugs him, he slowly warms to the gesture, and hugs her back, slightly smiling as he pats her on the back.

"Thank you. Thank you for your help," says Abeke.

"Yes! Thank you," says Tula as she watches them.

Abeke puts the bag on her shoulder and enthusiastically gets on the horse with Talako's help. Tula does the same, mounting the horse they had traveled with.

Talako takes a moment to look at the two girls, who smile back at him. The old man steps back and points north with his right hand. "Go in that direction. Stay under the cover of the trees, and away from the trails. After, you will come across the tracks of the large migration. I believe this is the group you are looking for. We will be right behind you."

Talako steps out of their way, and the girls begin to guide their horses through the native camp. They slowly make their way in the direction Talako pointed out to them. As they pass by families and elders, they smile and receive nods and smiles from the people on the ground. The girls finally exit the camp.

Talako stares in their direction for a little while after they leave, reflecting at what had just taken place, and hoping the girls will be safe.

*   *   *

Hours go by at Talako's camp. Afternoon turns into night rather quickly in these woods. Some members of his tribe have raised tents, others have fallen asleep close to one of the many fires they have going. Mothers keep their young ones nearby. Most have turned in for the night, save for a few warriors keeping watch. Crickets chirp, and frogs' croaks resound through the forest. The night is dark, and glimpses of stars can be seen through the heavy tree canopy above.

Talako stands up slowly, reaches over to the firewood, and puts another log on the fire. He slowly sits back down next to a group of men.

Chito, one of the young men sitting with him, observes as Talako sits back down and says, "You move slower than the turd I dropped in the woods yesterday, Talako…"

All the men chuckle as they look at Talako. Talako smiles with them and says, "You're so fast, your wife has become the tribal mule to get satisfied, everyone gets a ride."

All of the men break out in hysterical laughter, one even falling over to the side.

"No way! No way!" says Chito as everyone laughs.

A branch breaks in the forest close to camp, and everyone quickly quiets down and looks in that direction. Then, the sound of another broken stick is heard. Some of the men stand up, ready for a confrontation. They gesture to others sitting down, to get up and come closer. More sounds come from the forest. There is obvious movement. Something is coming their way. The men, now twenty of them, stand fast, holding their weapons as more join them. A mix of bows and arrows, spears and rifles await in steady hands.

Captain Francis and his native companion Abit slowly enter the native camp on horseback. Abit leads the way, his hands in the air, while the captain is vigorously scratching his arms and neck. His sleeves are rolled up, and it is apparent he is covered with a poison ivy rash. Abit looks around and nods at the native men pointing their weapons. The captain is a complete mess. His clothes are all out of place, his hair is ruffled, he is moving up and down his saddle, and he cannot stop scratching himself.

"Stop scratching," whispers Abit.

"I…I can't help it," replies the captain as he continues to scratch.

"I told you not to use that plant to wipe your ass. Now it's spreading," whispers Abit.

"The captain merely growls as he continues to scratch.

Abit and the captain stop their approach to the camp. Abit asks the captain, "Did you use the ointment I gave you?"

Abit turns around to see the captain's response, but Francis doesn't offer a word in return. His wild eyes and his continued scratching is all the response Abit needs.

Abit shakes his head and says, "Let me do the talking here and stay behind me."

Abit gets off his horse and looks around at the men of the tribe that are surrounding the two. He puts his weapons on the ground slowly, then takes a few steps back and raises his hands again.

Talako and the men of the camp slowly approach Abit, their weapons in hand. Talako leans over to the right to take a good look at the captain, now behind Abit, who is still on his horse, not paying attention to anything but his irritation. He sees the captain reaching into the back of his pants to scratch himself. He looks back at Abit, disgusted with the captain's behavior.

"Why are you here?" asks Talako.

"We don't mean any harm," says Abit. Abit sees that this is not a warm welcome. The men stare back at him without any change to their solid and somber expressions. "We would be willing to trade for information," says Abit.

"We know they came this way! Just tell us what direction they went!" yells the captain from his horse. Francis jumps down from the saddle with a nasty grimace. He sloppily walks over to Abit's side, but before he could keep going, Abit puts out his arm in front of him, preventing the captain from proceeding.

"Are we gonna have a problem here!" growls the captain.

All the warriors raise their weapons and point them at the captain, who seems unfazed as he stares at them in his foolish pride and arrogance.

Talako looks at Abit in the eye and says, "Take your white and leave."

The captain, like an unrestrained animal, twitches, slaps his hands and says, "Tell us where they went, damn it!"

Abit turns to the captain, who continues to scratch himself unmercifully. He pushes the captain backward; the captain is surprised and quickly becomes angry.

"You fool, get back on your horse!" says Abit. He pushes the resisting captain back a few more times and walks him back to his horse.

As the captain stands next to his horse, hesitant to get on, he says, "What the hell is wrong with you? We need to know where they went!"

Abit puts both of his hands on the captain's shoulders and slightly smiles. "I know exactly where they went," says Abit.

"What? " asks the captain.

Abit looks over at the men pointing their weapons and then tells the captain, "There are two sets fresh horse tracks leading from just a few feet away, all the way to the back of their camp. They've been here. These people gave them a horse." The captain looks over at the men pointing their weapons at them then looks back at Abit who quickly says, "Get on your horse, we're leaving the way we came. We'll circle around their perimeter and pick up their tracks on the other side… We're done here."

The captain's eyes glare up with excitement. He nods his head in approval, looks Abit right in the eye as he gets really close to him, and whispers, "That's why I love you..."

Abit and the captain mount their horses. They look at the natives who have not moved an inch, still holding their weapons high in the air, ready to strike. They turn their horses around and slowly exit the camp the same way they entered. The horses disappear into the forest and the natives slowly relax and lower their weapons. After a few minutes as all the people begin to get back to their bonfires, Talako continues to stand and look into the forest.

A young boy comes up to him and stands beside him. The boy asks, "What is it grandpa? What do you see?"

"The spirit of vengeance..." says Talako.

Before he could finish his sentence, two very large yellow cat eyes appear in the forest behind large shrubberies. The eyes look directly at Talako and the boy. The two stare, frozen in that spot. The large eyes begin to move, and a large mountain lion's head pops up out of the shrubs. The lion looks around, then looks at Talako one last time. It turns and silently follows the trail that the captain and Abit are on.

The young boy grabs onto Talako's leg in fear as he sees the tremendously large body of the lion.

Talako puts his hand on the boys back and comforts him. "It will not hurt us," Talako says.

"How do you know?" The boy asks.

"He is on a divine mission and will not rest until he has accomplished that task," Talako replies.

*   *   *

The following day, miles away, the large migrating party slowly makes its way through thick mud. It has been raining for hours, and it is still pouring, together with very strong winds. The weather makes the thousands of people's journey that much tougher. Lightning brightens the dark skies, and it travels in and out of the clouds above. A few moments later the thunder rolls, making young ones cry.

A native man leans to the side of his horse and vomits but continues as if nothing happened. Sickness is running rampant through the migrants. People moan, and babies cry. The wagons creak as they move from side to side, and the slurry of mud beneath them grabs the wheels then slowly releases them as they turn. The people cough and sneeze as they travel, some covered in wet blankets, others with no clothes at all, leaving everyone wet.

Isi sits next to Biisan as he drives Jean's wagon, both as soaked as the rest of the procession. Their hearts sink in their chests as they see the people struggling to move. Biisan wipes his face, but it is really for nothing because the falling rain is so thick that it does not make a difference. They sit in silence as they watch people fall into the mud, and get up, only to fall again.

"I never thought that I would be here," Biisan said, drawing a curious glance from Isi. He continued, "My father was an elder in the Coushatta tribe. I grew up at a time where our world was becoming intertwined with the

white man, and conflicts were brewing all over our land.
My father traded furs with the French and gave to me
knowledge of the complexity of navigating between
different worlds.

"I grew up learning not only the traditions and the
values of my people and our heritage, but also many of the
customs and the language of the French traders my father
worked with. My father tried to be the bridge between the
white man and our people. My father was very smart. He
was intelligent and was able to adapt to the many changes
that were coming.

"But the greed of the white man is endless, like the
waters of the ocean—like the stars in the sky. There is no
end to what they want to take. My father foresaw many
years ago that the future of my tribe, and my future, was to
live differently than our ancestors, so that we could survive.

"By the time Jean came onto the scene my father
was very old, and he knew that we were at the brink of
losing it all. Year after year, land was taken by the white
man. People disappeared, we were not safe in our own

homeland, and we moved many times to try and live in peace.

"My father encouraged me to learn under Jean. He wanted me to learn the ways of the white man so that I could survive. My mother and the other elders were against it. He suggested Jean because he had earned my father's trust through good business, and fairness down through the last years of his life.

"I always wanted to help my people, and when I look around, I don't see differences from tribe to tribe, because the white man doesn't see differences among us. To them, we are all dogs—animals that need to be moved from one place to another.

"We must help ourselves and stick together. Each step away from my ancestral land feels like a loss of identity, and of my history. I feel isolated, torn between trying to help these people to safety, and not knowing what the future of my tribe I leave behind will be."

Isi is captivated by Biisan's story and asks, "How long have you been with Jean? Is he good?"

Biisan looks up at the dark sky, and lightning shines from behind the clouds. A few moments later, as the thunder is heard up above, Biisan replies, "I've worked with Jean for a few years. He treats me with respect, he's been good to me. It is a good thing that your path crossed with his."

Jean rides up the right side of the wagon on his horse and looks at Biisan and Isi. He is about to say something, but before he can open his mouth, everyone's attention is pulled away. There's a commotion up ahead, a lot of movement in the bushes to the right side of the trail. A woman screams and points into the bushes.

Jean rides up to the commotion. He looks at the woman pointing and then turns his horse into the bushes and rides a few yards into the woods. He finds a young native boy in a tug of war with a dog over a piece of cured pork. Jean smiles at first, finding the whole scene rather humorous, but then he sees there is something else in the bushes behind the boy, something very big.

Jean looks at the boy and says, "Let it go, son. Let's get back to the group."

The dog takes the pork from the boy's hand and runs away. The boy falls forward and quickly gets up and gives chase. They both run deeper into the forest. Jean shakes his head and follows behind them on his horse. He quickly catches up to the two, and in a small, secluded area he sees the dog finishing up the piece of meat while the boy screams at the dog and threatens him with a stick.

The boy cries, "You stupid dog, you ate the last of my meat. I should kill you and eat you, you stupid dog!"

The bushes behind the dog begin to move slightly.

Jean sees it and tell the boy, "Let's go, son! Let it be! Get on my horse now!"

The boy looks at Jean, still distressed about the pork, when suddenly a wolf jumps out of the bushes and grabs the dog by the throat, taking it down to the ground in one pounce. The boy is startled and falls backward. Jean's horse rears and takes a few steps back. Another wolf jumps out, and positions itself between the boy and the dog being killed. The wolf growls at the boy. Jean turns around and sees that there is another wolf coming up from the rear, leaving them surrounded. His horse grows restless, moving from side to side and kicking the air as the wolf approaches.

Jean holds on to his horse's reins tight and tries to calm his horse by petting his neck. Jean looks around and knows their situation is dire. The wolf behind Jean creeps a little bit closer, too close for Jean's taste. He nudges his horse and quickly makes his way to the boy. Jean rides past the wolves and when he is right beside the boy, he grabs the boy's right arm and quickly throws him on his lap. As he rides back to the trail, he sees the wolves following behind. They hear the dog crying loudly as the wolf finally kills it.

Jean leans forward, holding onto the boy as he rides. He looks back and sees the wolves. They are trailing not far behind. Suddenly, another wolf flanks Jean, it comes out of the woods from John's right side, grabs the boy's ankle and pulls him from John's lap. The boy falls to the ground and is quickly dragged by the wolf into the woods. John immediately stops his horse and turns around. Two wolves stand in front of him, facing him and standing in between him and the boy as the other wolf continues to drag him deeper into the woods. The wolves growl as the boy is heard beyond the bushes screaming for help.

Jean looks at the wolves as they slowly approach him, pulls out his rifle and says, "I see you don't like your life. I can help you with that."

Jean proves to be an excellent shot, hitting the first wolf right between the eyes with his musket. The other wolf runs and jumps toward him. Jean quickly drops the musket and grabs his Harper's Ferry flintlock pistol from the holster on his hip. The wolf leaps toward him, and Jean takes him down with one shot to the heart.

The boy continues screaming, his voice growing fainter. Jean rides into the woods after him.

Meanwhile, back on the trail, Isi sits alone on the bench of the stopped wagon, completely drenched by the heavy rain that keeps coming down. She looks around and sees Biisan a bit further down the trail looking for Jean, when suddenly a wolf plops down beside her. Startled, she jumps up and sees Jean on his horse with the boy sitting behind him. He takes another wolf from his lap and throws it on top of the other one.

"What's this?" asks Isi.

"Dinner," says Jean.

Isi looks at the wolves beside her, and then looks at the boy sitting on Jean's horse. The boy grins but is covered in blood. As the adrenaline subsides from his body, he slowly closes his eyes and falls of the horse.

Jean looks down at the boy, then at Isi and says, "Let's get him some help."

The two quickly pick up the boy and bring him into the wagon. Isi takes a closer look at the boy. "The wound is deep, but he will heal," says Isi.

Chapter 7: Delicacies

The sky is gray, and a light drizzle begins to fall on Abeke and Tula as they make their way through the forest, the Mississippi river just a few yards away. The clouds are so low they seem to be touching the top of the trees. A heavy fog begins to set in from the north. Summer is fleeting, and the weather is changing. The girls can feel it in the wind, no longer a warm breeze, but sharp cool bursts of wind hit them as they travel. Bird calls are heard in the distance and echo throughout the land. The girls move, one behind the other, covered in blankets. On their horses, they slowly ride, fighting against the cold wind that faces them.

"Tula?" Abeke asks.

"Yes?" replies Tula.

"When we find your sister, do you think she will accept me?" asks Abeke.

Tula slows her horse down and allows Abeke to get beside her. She looks at Abeke in the eyes and asks, "Why would you ask me something like that?"

Abeke is a little apprehensive about answering. She looks down, grabs the horn of the saddle tightly, and then says, "I would like for us to stay together. I've been separated from everyone I love, all my life. For once I would like someone I love to stay in my life. You…you've become like a sister to me. I would like it very much if you could stay in my life. I've grown to love you. My heart really cares for you, and I would love for my child to get to know you. Maybe when you grow up some more and have kids, I could also be their aunt."

There are a few seconds of silence. Abeke continues to look down as the horses continue to walk and says, "Don' mind me. I think about stupid stuff like that sometimes. Forget what I just said," she tries to ease the tension with a laugh. Abeke looks out into the forest or a few seconds, then looks back at Tula. To her surprise, Tula is crying. Tears are pouring out of her eyes, and her lips are quivering. "What? I'm sorry…" says Abeke.

Suddenly Tula reaches out and hugs her tightly, so much so, that she almost comes off her horse.

"You *are* my sister!" says Tula. "Isi will love you just as much as I do, if not more, because she's the nice one. And you will stay with us, and live with us, and eat with us!"

Abeke smiles. She too becomes emotional and begins to tear up.

"We will help you raise your baby, and regardless of whether it's a boy or a girl, the child will grow up to be a warrior! You'll see! We will all grow old together. We'll be old ladies sitting in front of a fire telling our grandchildren about our journey north!" says Tula.

Abeke hugs Tula back, then gently helps her get situated back in the saddle. The girls look at each other for a few moments as their horses slowly move forward.

"Don't you feel it? Our spirits have been woven together. You are my sister forever!" says Tula.

"Forever…" says Abeke as she smiles.

The girls continue to travel side by side, the fog completely surrounding them now. Visibility is so difficult, they can't see more than a few feet in front of them.

"Maybe we should stop until the fog clears?" asks Abeke.

"It's ok. As long as we keep the river to our right, we'll know we're going north."

Suddenly Abeke hold her hand up and says, "Wait! Did you hear that?"

Tula stops her horse and listens. "Yeah, what is that?"

The girls draw their horses to a stop and listen.

"Sounds like somebody moaning," says Abeke.

"I think it's coming from the river," says Tula.

Slowly they approach the riverbank. Their horses navigating through trees and brush makes the water resting on the leaves splatter on them as they pass through. The girls come out of the wet forest and look around to see where the sound is coming from.

"Look!" says Tula as she points upriver.

"Is that…?"

"Yeah, it looks like someone halfway in the water waving at us, they're yelling something, but I can't make it out."

The girls look at each other, then to the person in the distance.

"Should we go and help?" asks Tula.

"Let's see what's going on."

The two move their horses up the riverbank. As they draw closer, they see that it's an older man that was waving at them. The man looks to have one of his feet stuck underneath a large boulder. He is sitting in the water, one foot on the boulder, the other underneath it. He waves at the girls, with a large smile.

"Thank God you came!" the man said.

The tall white man looks to be in his mid-fifties. He is bald and has a long shaggy beard. He's dressed in old, tattered clothing with holes everywhere.

"Please help me out! My foot is stuck underneath this boulder here, and I can't get it out! I've tried everything! Ouch…ouch, this hurts."

The girls stay on their horses, not knowing what to think. As they look around, they see a horse tied up to a tree nearby.

"Yeah, that's my horse. His name is Marvin," says the man.

"What's your name, mister?"

The man splashes in the water as he tries to get a grip and pull himself out. He stops, leans back, looks at the girls and says, "My name's Grady. Grady Hunt. Hey, could you girls give me a hand here, please?"

Abeke and Tula look at each other, then back at Grady, apprehensive about helping him.

"This water's cold. If I don't get outta here, I'ma die!"

"How did you get stuck in there? I'm sure that big rock didn't fall from nowhere," asks Abeke.

Grady tries to pull himself out again, putting his free foot on the boulder. He pushes but fails and flops back down on the water. "I was standing on this boulder here, I was taking a look around, but I slipped and fell, and my foot went under. There's suction, and I can't get any leverage to pull myself out."

There's a long pause. Finally Tula gets off her horse and Abeke follows. Grady smiles. The girls take their blankets and place them on their horses.

"Yes, please help. I promise I'm just a good man in a bad situation," Says Grady.

They approach Grady cautiously, and stop about six feet away from him.

"Look mister, we'll help you, but you gotta promise not to try anything on us afterwards," says Abeke.

Grady looks at the girls as if insulted and says, "Now, I'm not that type of person! I promise, I… I promise that if you help me get outta here I will be most grateful, and I will give you some of my provisions."

"What?" asks Tula.

"I got a little cabin not too far from here. I don't have much, but I will share what I got with you. Please, please help me?"

The girls look at each other for a moment, then Tula says, "We don't want nothing from you, we'll help you get out, and we'll be on our way."

"Okay, sounds good to me!" says Grady.

Abeke and Tula walk toward the man as he reaches for them.

"One of you take this hand, while I try to stand, the other helps me get up and out of the mud pit under this rock," says Grady.

Abeke takes Grady's hand and Tula gets behind him and grabs him underneath his armpits.

"Ready! One…two…three…*pull*!" says Grady.

The girls pull Grady with all their strength, and he pulls himself with his hands, and pushes with his one free foot, until finally, his foot comes out from underneath the boulder. They all fall backward into the water. Grady quickly gets up, and helps the girls stand to their feet.

"Thank you! Thank you, young ladies! You have been so kind in helping me!" says Grady as he helps them up. He escorts the girls out of the water saying, "Come on.

Come on, get out of that cold water. Thank you, thank you girls!"

The girls begin to walk back to their horses, but Grady says, "Wait, wait. I never got your names…"

The two turn around, and Abeke says, "This is Tula, I'm Abeke."

Grady gestures his gratitude by mimicking a hug, then puts his hands on his heart and says, "What wonderful names. Now, now you have to let me do something nice for you. After all, you two saved my life!"

"We best be on our way," says Tula as the two walk away.

Grady runs after them, puts his hands in a praying position and pleads with them saying, "Please, please. At least let me give you some food. I have a warm chicken stew sitting over the fire. It's got potatoes and some carrots. I even put salt in it. It's so good."

"A warm meal sure sounds nice," says Abeke. She looks at Tula, who gently shakes her head 'no'. The light drizzle turns into a heavy rain.

Grady takes the opportunity to walk to his horse and take the reins. As he walks into the woods, he calls out to the girls, "Come on, let's get out of this rain. Follow me!"

Wanting to go, Abeke pouts her lips and looks at Tula.

Frustrated, Tula grabs the reins of her horse and says, "Fine, let's go. But keep your eyes open."

The girls follow Grady as he travels through the thick forest. The rain has intensified, and it's cold.

After a good fifteen minutes of walking, Grady looks back at the girls and says, "Just behind those trees there!"

The girls look past the trees and see a small, cozy cabin, with a plume of smoke coming out of the chimney.

Grady takes his horse under a makeshift shelter beside the house.

"Bring me your horses, go in the house and get out of the rain!" he says.

The girls hand over the horses to Grady, and quickly run into the house. When they walk in they see a nicely decorated cabin, with animal furs on the walls and on the floor. There are a few windows and a nice fireplace. There's a little bit of furniture: a table with a few chairs, and a cabinet by one of the windows with countertop, that's supposed to be a kitchen. To the left and right of the fireplace are two doors. One of them is closed, the other is open, and a small bedroom can be seen. The girls look around and see a framed picture of a woman and two little girls standing front of the very house they are in. This picture sits on a table by the window, and underneath the table there are a few children's toys. A large pot of stew hangs from a chain in the fireplace emitting a wonderful aroma that fills the house.

Grady opens the door, and comes in. The girls turn around, startled by the sudden entrance.

"Oh, I'm sorry girls. I didn't mean to scare you. I don't mind if you're looking around, that's perfectly okay," says Grady.

"Is that your family?" asks Abeke as she points to the family pictures.

Grady looks for a few seconds, then says, "Yes, that's my family."

"Where are they?" asks Tula.

"The passed away last year," answers Grady.

"I'm sorry," says Abeke.

Grady walks over to the back bedroom. He can be heard moving things around back there. "Yeah, they passed away last year!" he calls out from the other room. Then he comes back into the main room holding blankets and clothes. He puts everything down on the table and looks at the girls.

"What happened to them?" asks Tula.

"What?" says Grady.

"Your wife, and your little ones. How did they die?" asks Abeke.

"Oh…yeah. They got sick. Something made them really ill while I was away on some business. When I got home after a few weeks, I found them all dead in the house," said Grady.

"So sad," says Tula.

Grady, wanting to change the subject puts his hand on the table and says, "Well, I got some blankets and a change of clothes for you. You can use that bedroom there to get comfortable while I get your supper ready."

The girls nod, take the clothing and walk into the bedroom. Tula closes the door. The bedroom is small, with a small bed, a small desk and a wardrobe. Abeke looks through the clothes in the wardrobe.

"This must have been his oldest daughter's room; these are all girls' clothing," says Abeke.

Tula walks up to Abeke and whispers in her ear, "Something is not right here. I don't trust him."

"He's just trying to repay the favor. We did help him get out from underneath that rock, right?" Abeke whispers.

"I don't know, things are not sitting right in my heart. We should leave, now," says Tula

Abeke puts her hands on Tula's shoulder and says, "Okay. Let's change clothes, eat, and then we excuse ourselves, walk out the door, get on our horses and go."

Hesitantly, Tula nods and begins to get undressed. Abeke unfolds the fresh clothing on the bed. A few minutes later the girls open the bedroom door and come out wearing dresses. Grady immediately looks their way and smiles. He has also changed his clothes and is waiting for them at the table with bowls filled with stew.

"There you are! Now isn't that better? Come, come!" says Grady as he beckons them to the table.

The girls walk to the table. The smell of the stew is overwhelmingly good. The girls smile as they sit, and they both look at Grady.

"Thank you for helping me today and thank you for allowing me to do something nice for you. Doing good to people just nourishes me on the inside, and I hope it does the same for you," says Grady.

He opens a small cloth bundle sitting in front of him and takes out a loaf of bread. He cuts a thick slice and give it to Tula, sitting to his left.

"Look, I even have a loaf of bread. Here you go," says Grady with a smile.

The girls hold their spoon in one hand, and a piece of bread in the other, and look at Grady. Grady picks up his spoon, and begins to eat, the girls immediately following suit.

"This is really good!" says Abeke.

"I never tasted anything like this. It's delicious!" says Tula.

The girls can't help themselves. The stew is so good, they put spoonful after spoonful into their mouths. Grady slowly eats, as he watches the girls speed feeding their faces.

"So where are you girls going to?" asks Grady.

Abeke swallows, and says, "We're meeting our sister up north."

"I see. Well, I spotted a very large group of people, hundreds—no thousands of natives and many soldiers traveling north a few days ago. Is she with them?" asks Grady.

"Yes! She is with them. You saw them?" asks Tula.

Grady puts his hand on the table, and says, "I sure did. Just west of this cabin you'll see the trail they left. It's pretty remarkable. You can't miss it."

"Well, we have to go! We have to go find it!" says Tula as she puts the spoon down on the table.

"Now hold on, hold on. Don't do anything in haste. Be a little smart here. It's still raining cats and dogs out there, and it will probably rain throughout the night. Why don't you girls just finish your food, relax, you can spend the night get some rest in that bedroom over there. In the morning, we can saddle up, and I'll take you to the trail myself, say our goodbyes and you'll be on your way. What do you say?" says Grady.

The girls look at each other for a few seconds, then look back at Grady.

"Sounds good to me!" says Abeke.

"I guess… Hey how did you and your family end up out here?" asks Tula.

Grady takes the pot and refills their bowls with stew. He sits back down on his chair and reclines before he tells them the tale.

"Well, I used to be a teacher down in Louisiana. I lived in a small room with my wife Ethel, and my two little girls. We did not have a lot of money. I was struggling to put food on the table. The parish's school didn't pay much. One day, Mr. Allen, one of my co-workers, he told me about a place he had found, and that there was gold in a nearby cave. He needed help, someone he could trust to help him get the gold out. The cave is actually just a mile, mile and a half away from here. Anyways, we came out here last summer, and we looked at the cave and sure enough there was a gold vein in there. We were so excited. I'll never forget that day. I came back home, told Ethel and the girls, and we came out here. We built this cabin, Ethel planted a vegetable garden, everything was fine. Winter came, it got so cold and damp in there, we were making little progress in the cave. We decided to wait through the winter and begin work on the mine in the spring. Unfortunately, Allen got sick in January and died. My wife got sick after that, and so did my girls. I went back to

Louisiana to get some medicine, and when I came back, they were all gone. My whole family…"

The girls look at Grady, speechless, not knowing what to say.

"It's been a few months now; they're all buried out back," says Grady.

"So, what are you going to do now?" asks Tula, as her eyes slowly begin to close.

Seeing that the girls have finished eating, Grady gets up and takes their bowls from the table and places them on the kitchen counter on the side of the room.

"To be honest, I will probably just go back to Louisiana and try to find work as a teacher again. If I can find someone that can help me get that gold, I would gladly share it with them. But…I don't know."

Abeke looks over at Tula, her head is tilted all the way forward in her seat. She is dozing off to sleep. She realizes then that she herself feels very tired. She can hardly keep her eyes open. Her whole body feels like it's shutting down. She looks over at Grady who is wide awake, smiling at her.

"Why am I so sleepy? I can hardly stay awake… What's going on here?"

"You had a long day, better you get some rest," says Grady.

Abeke tries to stand. She pushes her chair back, but when she puts her weight on her legs, they shake underneath her and she falls to the floor.

"What did you do?" asks Abeke as she tries to crawl, her eyelids closing on her.

"Don't fight it. Just…go to sleep," says Grady.

"Wha…wha…" says Abeke before closing her eyes completely.

*   *   *

Abeke slowly opens her eyes. Her vision is blurry, and her head feel like it's been kicked by a horse. She tries to put her hand on her head, and she realizes she's in chains, shackled to the wall behind her. Abeke sits up and sees that her feet are also in chains. Looking around, she sees Tula on the other side of the dimly lit room. She is also in chains. The room looks like a storage closet. There are a lot of shelves with provisions.

"Tula. Tula, wake up!" whispers Abeke, but Tula does not respond.

Abeke looks around, and in the corner of the room she sees another person sitting in the shadows.

"Hello?" Abeke asks, but there is no answer.

Abeke shifts her weight and looks into the dark corner from a different angle. She can make out a female figure sitting against the wall.

"Hey, are you ok?" Abeke asks.

"Be quiet!" says the girl in the corner.

Abeke becomes intrigued, and tries to get up, but can't because of the chains.

"Stop making noise, or he'll come in here and beat you," says the girl.

Abeke looks over at Tula, still sleeping.

"Is that your friend?" asks the girl in the shadows.

"That's my sister. You've been in here the whole time? Who are you? Where are we?" asks Abeke.

Out of the shadows pops out a girl's face. She's a bushy-haired, red-headed girl with pretty blue eyes and pale white skin, filled with freckles. She's no more than twenty years old.

"He got you with the foot underneath the boulder bit, didn't he?" asks the girl.

Abeke looks over at Tula again, remembering her warnings about not staying. Abeke looks over at the girl in the shadows and says, "Yeah… That's how he got us here."

"That son of a bitch!" says the girl, before she disappears back into the shadows.

Abeke, looking in the direction the girl disappeared, asks, "Is that how he got you too?"

There is only silence. The girl does not respond. Abeke looks in the opposite direction and sees a door behind some shelving units loaded with supplies. She looks over at Tula again, still sleeping.

"That's how he got my father," the girl in the shadows finally says.

Abeke quickly turns and looks into the shadows but can't see her.

"This is *my* house," says the girl.

Abeke hears her voice coming from a different direction. She sees the girl now, sitting beside Tula. The girl is completely naked and dirty. She has a metal ring around her neck with a long chain attached to it. She's missing her left leg right up to the thigh. The wound is completely healed so it must have happened a while ago. The girl begins to pet Tula's hair and gently moves it from her face.

"You're not the first, and probably won't be the last. He got a man, a traveler, the same way last week," says the girl.

"What happened to him?" asks Abeke.

After a long pause, the girl whispers, "You ate him last night."

Abeke is completely disgusted. She squirms and says, "What the hell!"

"Be quiet, or it's gonna get bad for you," warns the girl.

Abeke looks down at her chained feet. She can't believe her predicament. How did she end up in chains again? There's got to be a way out of here, she thinks. This cannot be the end. She looks at the girl and asks, "What's your name? And what do you mean this is your house?" asks Abeke.

The girl looks at Abeke, her bright blue eyes seem to pierce the darkness of the room.

"My name is Rebecca Vaughn. And yes, this is my house. My family moved out here years ago. That picture you saw in the large room? That's my mom, my older sister and me. My father never liked taking pictures, so he was never in one. It made it easier for Grady to tell his story. My father moved us out here. He wanted land—a homestead. He wanted us to grow up out in the open. We were happy for a while. My father would hunt and fish. My mother would give us school lessons, and she planted a garden.

"One day, my dad brought Grady home. Said he found him by the river, with his leg caught underneath a boulder. We felt so bad for him. He came across as a very nice man. He said he was a schoolteacher in Louisiana and was traveling east to meet his family. Fucking liar. We fed him and let him stay the night. Woke up the next morning tied up. He slit my father's throat in his sleep. He raped my mother, my sister and I, and kept us locked up in this here room."

"What happened to your mother and sister?" asks Abeke.

"He kept raping them until they got pregnant. I was too young to get pregnant then. My older sister gave birth to a son, and soon after that, so did my mother. As soon as the babies were weaned, he took them away."

"Where? Where did he take the babies?" asks Abeke.

"I didn't know at the time. All I know is that he just took them. Months turned to years. He kept us in this room and kept impregnating my mother and sister. After a few years, I got pregnant myself," says Rebecca.

"How old were you?" asks Abeke.

Rebecca looks down at her midsection and paces her hands on her belly.

"I must have been ten or eleven years old," says Rebecca.

Abeke puts her hands on her own pregnant belly, fearing what Grady may do to the child. She looks up and sees Rebecca looking at her with pity and concern.

"I'm afraid to ask… Your mom and sister?" Abeke presses.

Rebecca looks away and says, "My sister was giving birth to her eleventh child. My mom, pregnant herself, was helping her with the delivery. Grady kept me back here tied up, but I could hear everything. He just stood by the door with a large knife in his hand, popped his head in to check on me every now and then.

"But something went wrong. The baby was not coming out, and she was bleeding really bad. Sometime during the night, my sister stopped breathing. I could hear my mother screaming at her, telling her to breathe. Next thing I know, Grady threw my mom back in here and chained her up. She couldn't stop crying. My sister was dead, and the baby was still inside her."

Rebecca points to a little hole in the wall right above her, and continues to speak,

"I saw the whole thing through that hole right there. Grady went to the table and cut that baby out of my sister. The baby cried and seemed fine. He wrapped it up and put it on the counter. Then he began to cut my sister up into pieces, he separated her legs, her arms—it was horrible. He took her outside. It was winter and it was very cold, so he must have kept the body out there so it would not decompose. The next day baby was gone. He took it.

"He made us eat my sister over time. He threatened to kill us if we didn't eat. My mom was not the same after that. She was not able to focus on anything. She always seemed like she was thinking about something. Her mind was far away from the here and now. A few months later, she gave birth to her child, and she didn't even cry. She kneeled on the ground and pushed that baby out of her.

When the baby fell from her body, she chewed through the umbilical cord, stood up, and walked back into this room, like nothing had happened. She just left the baby in a small pool of blood crying on the floor, didn't even look at it. Grady was even taken aback by it. He came back here, put the chains on her and closed the door.

"What he forgot to do that time was to lock the door. He was so shocked by my mother's behavior, he had forgotten. And he had me chained up with a single fetter around my right wrist. When I saw him wrap that baby up and walk out the door, I wanted to follow him. I was able to slip my hand out of those chains, and I went out the door. It was weird exiting the house after so many years. I saw him going into the woods in the distance, and I followed. My plan was to see where the babies were going, and then leave and get help for my mom. After a few miles, I remember him meeting a group of men gathered in a camp by the river. The night was very bright, because there was a full moon out. I was hiding way back in the trees so they could not see me.

"One of the men got up from sitting by the large fire and walked up to Grady. Grady handed him the baby, and they gave him money. He had been selling our children all along. I was so upset, it burned in my gut. I could not stand it anymore. I slowly began to back away, when all of a sudden, I felt somebody's hand fall on my shoulder. When I turned around to look, a big, burly, bearded man grabbed me and picked me up. I couldn't help but scream. I was so afraid. He brought me to where Grady and the other men were standing and threw me on the ground in front of them.

"You stupid little bitch!" screamed Grady.

"The man that gave the money to Grady took a very large knife from his side, and put it right into the flame. He goes into a large bag, takes out a hatchet and gives it to Grady.

"He told Grady that the men were hungry, and that it would be dangerous for him to have their milch cow running off on him. They told him he knew what to do."

Rebecca grows quiet for a few seconds. Pain and resentment grip her heart. A few tears begin to fall from her eyes, but she musters the strength to continue to say, "They cut my leg off and ate it right in front of me."

Abeke shakes her head and says, "Monsters! Those men are monsters!" says Abeke.

Rebecca wipes her tears and continues to tell her story.

"The next morning, Grady threw me over his shoulder and brought me back to the cabin. When he brought me into this room, my mom didn't say a word to me. My leg was missing, and she didn't even look at me. That's when I knew her mind was gone. I tried talking to her, even screamed at her, but it was like she was not there. A few weeks went by, and Grady got us pregnant again. When my mom began to show, something got triggered inside her. She began to bang her head against the wall. She would bang her head so hard sometimes I thought the whole cabin was shaking. Grady would come in here and wrap her head up in blankets, but she would find a way to take them off and bang her head. If it wasn't the wall, it was the floor.

"The morning that I gave birth to my child, when Grady brought me back here to chain me up, we found my mother in a pool of blood. In all her headbanging, she had exposed a large nail, and she banged her head several times against it. The nail went right through her skull. That was about a month ago."

Rebecca reaches into the dark corner, and then tosses a four-inch nail in front of Abeke's feet. "Grady pulled the nail out and gave it to me, I don't know why."

Abeke, with her mouth open, looks at Rebecca without saying a word.

"That's a horrible story!" says Tula.

Rebecca and Abeke are startled by the sudden interruption.

"Tula! How long have you been awake?" asks Abeke.

"Long enough to know we need to get out of here," says Tula

In that very moment, the door slams open. Grady looks in, smiles and says, "I see you're getting acquainted, very good, very good!"

Grady enters the little room and walks up to Rebecca. "It's time, Becca. Come on sweetheart, you know the drill."

"Yeah..." says Rebecca.

"Leave her alone!" yells Abeke.

"Stop! Stop it!" screams Tula as Grady takes the chain of Rebecca's neck.

Rebecca does not fight back. She is completely defeated. As the girls watch Grady pick her up and throw her onto his shoulder, they can tell by the look on her face, that Rebecca has surrendered to her fate. Grady takes her out of the room. He closes the door behind him and locks it.

"What are we going to do?" asks Tula.

"I don't know, but I have a feeling that you're next," says Abeke.

"Why would you say that?" asks Tula.

"I already have a baby inside me Tula." Says Abeke.

Tula looks at Abeke's belly, then looks at the door in fear. She beings to look for a way out and pulls on her chains. Through the wall, the girls hear Grady moaning and grunting, and a lot of knocking around.

"I've got to get out of here. I've got to get out of here!" says Tula, over and over.

"We have to think of something!" says Abeke.

"When he comes back in, I'll trip him, and you hit him over the head with something. Then we get the keys to these chains and get out of here!" says Tula.

Abeke looks around. At the bottom of one of the shelving units, she sees a large metal bucket. She quickly grabs it and puts it right beside her. The girls look at each other, and nod in agreement.

Grady's grunting comes to an end, and then there is silence in the other room. The girls look at each other with fear and perk their ears up as they hear footsteps coming toward them. Suddenly the door opens, and Grady comes in naked, holding Rebecca over his shoulder, with a keyring in his hand. With a smug smile, he brings the girl back to her dark end of the room and puts her down on the floor. Rebecca does not make eye contact with the girls, her face covered with shame.

As Grady reaches for the neck ring to put on Rebecca, Tula grabs his leg and tries to get him off balance. Grady stumbles back but he grabs onto one of the shelves and keeps his footing. He struggles to get Tula off of him because her hold is tight. She is not letting go of him. Grady finally smacks her in the face. Abeke throws the metal pot at Grady's head and hits him behind the left ear making a small cut.

"Ahh, you little bitch!" shouts Grady.

Grady kicks Tula off him, runs to Abeke, and punches her right in the face, knocking her unconscious and spilling her against the wall and to the floor.

"No!" screams Tula.

Grady reaches back and backhands Tula, so hard that she hits the wall behind her.

"You and I are gonna have ourselves a little fun right now," Grady tells Tula as he reaches for the keyring on the floor.

Grady unchains Tula as she kicks and punches him. He's having a hard time getting access to her so slaps her again to keep her from resisting. The slap is so hard that it gives her a nosebleed, and it dazes her to the point where it almost knocks her out.

Grady takes Tula under his arm like a sack of potatoes, walks out of the little room, and closes the door. He quickly makes his way to the table in the middle of the living room, and lays Tula on her back. Tula, still hurting and dazed from his slap, tries to gather herself, but can't really do anything. He ties her hands to the legs of the table and take her skirt off. He looks at Tula, who is now looking back at him, and he begins to masturbate.

"Wha…what are you doing?" asks Tula.

Grady walks around the table. He caresses Tula's face with one hand while pleasuring himself with the other. He then leans down to Tula, puts his face close to hers and says, "Today you're gonna know what it like to be a wom—ahh!"

In pain, Grady leans forward. Seeing the opportunity, Tula bites his throat, with all her might.

"Guh!" Screams Grady again, as his throat begins to bleed from Tula's bite.

With a shift of the eyes, Tula sees Rebecca has stabbed Grady in the leg using the nail that killed her mother. She climbs his body as a rock climber scales a cliff, stabbing him now in the back as she pulls herself up. She stabs him again in the lower back as she gets her foot securely on the floor. Then she stabs him again on his upper back, pulling herself now to a full standing position. Rage takes over Rebecca's countenance. The years of abuse and pain, like an erupting volcano, completely explode in a burst of emotions. She stabs Grady in his ear and his temple repeatedly as her screams echo through the cabin and into the wilderness outside.

Grady falls dead onto the floor, a pool of blood spilling out of his head. Rebecca looks at Tula, who still has a piece of Grady's throat in her mouth, and she hugs her.

Tula spits the flesh out of her mouth, leans in to receive the hug and says, "Thank you! Thank you!"

Rebecca quickly begins to free Tula, loosening the ropes that hold her arms down. Now free, Tula reaches up and hugs Rebecca tightly.

"Thank you. Thank you for saving me! How did you get free?" asks Tula.

"He was so concerned about you, that he forgot to lock me up, and he left the door unlocked as well. Right after he took you, I saw the nail that killed my mother on the floor. All I could think about was that I couldn't let you go through what I have gone through, I just couldn't… It had to end. Here, put your skirt back on," says Rebecca as she gives Tula her skirt.

Tula jumps off the table, and onto the floor. She puts her skirt back on and quickly grabs the keyring that Grady put on a chair. She runs into the little room and frees Abeke.

"Come on sis, wake up!" says Tula as she unlocks the chains binding Abeke.

Abeke slowly begins to come to. Tula quickly helps her sit up against the wall.

"How… What…" says Abeke.

"We killed him. We killed him, Abeke!" says Tula.

Tula helps Abeke get ton her feet, and slowly guides her out of the room. When they come out into the living room, Abeke sees Grady's body on the floor, laying in a pool of blood. Rebecca, sitting naked on one of the chairs, and covered in blood, looks at the girls as they enter the room. Tula helps Abeke to one of the chairs and helps her sit down. The girls look at Grady's body lying on the floor for a few minutes.

"You're free, Rebecca," says Tula.

Rebecca looks at Tula, take a deep breath, and tears begin to fall from her eyes. The realization of what she just said suddenly hits her. She leans forward and begins to cry uncontrollably. Tula quickly runs and places her hand on her back and tries to console her.

"So many years were stolen from me. So many babies were taken from me! Where are they? Where are my babies! You bastard!" Rebecca cries.

Abeke gets up, walks over to Rebecca, hugs her and begins to rock her back and forth to comfort her.

"We're here, honey. You got us, and we got you. You're not alone," says Abeke.

Rebecca looks at Abeke, and hugs her tightly. Tula can't help herself and hugs them both.

"Thank you…" says Rebecca.

The girls pull away, and smile at Rebecca

.

"Where are your clothes, Rebecca? I'll go get them for you," says Tula.

"You know, the last time I wore clothes…was ten years ago. He's kept me naked for years," says Rebecca.

"That son of a bitch!" says Abeke.

"Help me get this body outside, and then let's clean Rebecca up and get her some clothes," says Tula.

Tula and Abeke slowly drag Grady's body out the door. Rebecca grabs some rags on the countertop, slowly lets herself down onto the floor and begins to soak up the blood with the rags. After a little while, she looks around the cabin and contemplates on all the years she was kept captive here. It was over. The horrors in this cabin were finally over.

The girls walk back into the cabin and find Rebecca on the floor.

"What are you doing down there?" asks Abeke.

The girls quickly pick Rebecca off the floor and sit her down on a chair.

"I'm going to go and get some water. We're going to clean up."

Abeke walks toward the bedroom saying, "I'm getting you some clothes honey, and tomorrow, you're coming with us."

Rebecca slightly smiles.

Chapter 8: The Wilderness

The next afternoon, under a gray and cloudy sky, the three girls ready for travel sit on their horses and look at the cabin. Bird calls resonate throughout the forest. A slight drizzle begins to fall.

"You sure you want to do this?" asks Abeke.

"Yes… Yes I am," says Rebecca as she lights a makeshift torch.

She rides close to the cabin, throws the torch through the window, and slowly rides back. The cabin begins to burn—the floor inside first, then the walls and then the house quickly becomes engulfed in flames. The girls ride into the forest on their horses loaded with supplies, as the crackling of the burning wood bids them farewell. They continue to head north, keeping the river close to them.

A few hours go by, and the girls make their way out of the forest and into a large clearing. Wrapped in blankets and a little worn down, the girls notice the change in scenery. Tula stops her horse and jumps off. She looks at the ground and walks around, finding hundreds and hundreds of tracks.

"This is them," Tula excitedly says as she continues to walk back and forth from one side of the trail to the other.

Abeke and Rebecca look on as Tula's eagerness causes her to run back and forth from one side to the other of the wide span of tracks.

"This is it! We found them," Tula says, laughing mirthfully. "We found *her*!" She points north, where all of the tracks are headed and says, "They're all going in that direction!"

Rebecca rides her horse close to Tula, leans forward and asks, "What is all this?"

"These are old tracks. Several days old, in fact. But so many people, horses and wagons passed through here,

that the rain was not able to wash it all away. Enough of it
is here," says Tula as she kneels to get a better look.

"So, we're getting closer to your sister," says
Abeke.

"We just need to follow this trail here," says Tula as
she climbs back to her feet. "At least we know where to
go."

As Tula climbs atop her horse, she notices Rebecca
and Abeke looking at something on the side of the trail.
Tula turns to look and sees numerous mounds some
covered in stone. Others are simply made of dirt and soil.

"What are those?" asks Tula.

"Graves," says Rebecca.

"Graves?" Tula wonders.

The girls look around and see numerous mounds on
both sides of the trail.

"White folks bury their dead this way," says Abeke.

They approach a group of graves and see that the rain has washed some of the earth away, taking with it the trinkets and flowers that were originally placed on the mound.

"This is not our way…" says Tula.

Abeke suddenly groans, sucking air through her gnashed teeth as she bends over in pain, holding her belly.

Rebecca puts her hand on Abeke to keep her from falling off her horse.

"Oh. Ooh, it's coming!" cries Abeke

"Let's find a place to make camp," Tula urges.

Tula leads Abeke and Rebecca off the trail and into the woods. They find a small clearing with a fallen tree. Rebecca slowly lets herself down off her horse. Tula help Abeke off her horse and they both lay her up against the log.

"Ahh. Ooh," Abeke moans as she leans back.

Rebecca sits in front of Abeke, and tells Tula, "We're going to need some of those blankets on my horse. Let's get her some water."

Tula runs to the horse, gets the blankets, and brings them back to Rebecca.

"Ahh, is the baby coming?" screams Abeke.

Rebecca takes a closer look at Abeke. She peers under her dress and says, "Just relax… Rest, it's just a false alarm."

"How do you know?" asks Tula.

Rebecca looks at Tula stoically, without saying a word.

"Right," Tula says. "Right, you have plenty of experience. Thank you… I'll…I'll get the water."

Tula runs back to the horses, gets all the canteens, and brings them back to Rebecca.

"Thank you. Just lay them down over here. We'll be here for a while," says Rebecca.

Tula looks up, and sees that it's getting dark, and says, "I better make a fire for us."

*   *   *

At the same exact time, miles away, Jean adds another log onto his fire, then sits on a little stool as he watches the flames dance. The embers travel high into the dark, cloudy sky. Not one star shines through the overcast haze above. His wagon sits behind him, the horses tied to a nearby tree, and he has set up a canopy, just in case it begins to rain again. Biisan stirs something on a cast iron pot over the open fire. Jean takes his pipe and tobacco out of his jacket and begins to load his pipe.

"How long do you think we have until we get there?" asks Biisan.

"Well, the type of trees and the landscape we're seeing is changing, so we've made some progress. But where we're going, there's more nothing than anything else," says Jean as he lights his pipe.

"You've been there? What is it like?"

"I've passed by it in my travels north. It's barren land. No trees, the soil is worthless… The access to water is scarce. It's a hard place to live in," says Jean.

Jean looks over to the rest of the people in their encampments. He sees natives and soldiers walking to and fro in the large camp. People make food, get their sleeping arrangements sorted out, and feed their fires. A lot of them are sick, coughing and sneezing. He can hear crying and moaning.

On the other side of the trail, a group of soldiers and natives dig graves for the dead. The feelings of fear and misery hang heavy in the air. People are dying daily. If it's not the sicknesses going around, it's the weather, or exhaustion. A few small children run by Jean's camp, chasing each other, and for a moment, Jean feels a spark of hope for the people.

Isi walks into the camp holding a small leather bag.

"Did you get them?" asks Biisan.

Isi walks up to Biisan and hands him the bag. Biisan looks inside and smiles. He quickly begins to add the herbs into the stew. Isi observes as he stirs the pot, she then looks around and sees that the men are all alone.

"Where is everyone else?" asks Isi.

Jean takes a puff from his pipe and says, "Well, the old lady said she found a cousin of hers and decided to travel with them. I haven't seen Atepa and her son in a few hours now… Maybe she'll come back, maybe she won't."

"That's her name? Well, shouldn't we look for her?" Isi asks. Isi looks at Jean a bit bewildered, not understanding why he won't go looking for the young girl.

Jean sees that look in her eyes and says, "I don't hold people hostage. She wanted to go look for some relatives."

Isi looks at Jean in disbelief and says, "But it's dangerous!"

"I told her that," Jean says.

"She could get killed or lost!" says Isi.

"I told her that too…" says Jean.

"What will happen to her?" asks Isi.

Jean takes another draw from his pipe and says, "I don't know. There are hundreds of people on this trail, Isi. We can only help so many. She wanted to go, so she left. And if she wants to return, then I will be glad to help her."

Biisan takes the spoon and tastes the stew. He nods in approval and says, "It's just the three of us for now, we'll be ok."

Isi walk up to Jean and sits down beside him. Jean blows out smoke up into the night sky and turns to look at Isi, who is already looking at him.

"Thank you for helping me, you really are a good man," says Isi.

Jean takes another puff from his pipe, and says, "I'm not a good man. But whatever you see in me today, it wasn't always there."

Isi, wondering what he's talking about, asks, "What do you mean?"

"There was a time, when I was younger, when… Well let's just say I was definitely not a good man back then," says Jean.

"Jean we've all done, at one point or another—" Isi begins to say.

"I know," Jean interrupts. "I know. But I want you to know who I really am." When Isi nods in approval, Jean continues his story. "I told you that I grew up helping my father in his trading business. And that's true. What I didn't tell you is that from time to time, runaway slaves would enter into the lands we set our traps on. They did not know the land, or where to go. They knew nobody. I knew that there would be a prize on their head so when I came across one, instead of helping them escape, I delayed them with food and shelter until the hunters came looking for them."

"What?" says Isi.

"Hear me out. I was not a slaver, but I did help the hunting parties get slaves that escaped from time to time," says Jean.

"Why? You've showed me kindness. This is not the Jean I know…" says Isi.

A world of emotions flood Jean's heart, as this is a very hurtful topic for him. "I'm glad you see me that way now, but back then, the only thing that moved me was money. I was young and uncaring. You would be surprised what people will do for money."

Isi looks out into the camp, and as she looks at hundreds of native families and soldiers, she says, "No, I know exactly what people will do for money… What changed for you?"

Jean looks in the same direction as Isi is looking and says, "One man. It was when I met this one man. I still remember everything about that day. I was in the swamps of Louisiana at that time. The day is stamped in my mind. The sun rays broke through the tree canopy above and shined on the swamp below. Tall grasses were everywhere, mossy tree trunks and some of the nastiest green water you'll ever see. I was a lot younger then, and I was paddling my small boat toward the shore to check on some of my traps. When I got off the boat, I heard some noises coming from a nearby bush, so I quickly got my rifle and pointed in that direction. I was expecting some type of animal. A boar, maybe. Even a large cat of some kind. Well, out of nowhere, an older black man slowly comes out of the bushes. His hands were up, but he did not say anything to me. He was not begging for his life, or anything. He just looked at me and smiled.

"I asked him who he was and what he was doing out there. I mean, I used to go for weeks and not see a single soul in those swamps, so I wanted to know more. He told me his name was Thomas. Said he didn't have a last name, and sure enough, he was a runaway slave…"

Jean begins to see and experience the whole interaction in his mind: the way the sun hit the leaves, the sound of the frogs and the birds in the trees, the look on Thomas's face as he stood up—every little detail, every little nuance. He is reliving the moment as he relays the story to Isi. He sees his old cabin, adorned with his old pelts, and trophy animal heads on the walls. He sees the small wooden table with the old gas lamp in the middle of the room, the small chimney with the pot of stew hanging from a chain, and the small bed in the corner of the room. Jean sees himself entering the cabin through the small front door. He looks back, and through one of the small little windows, sees Thomas following him inside. Jean beckons for Thomas to sit at the table.

"Come on in. I will get you some new clothes here in a few, and I have a nice blanket you can use to get some sleep. Hey, I got some hot stew ready, would you like some?" asks Jean.

Thomas sits at the table and looks around the cabin. But he nods to Jean. "Yes, please. I would love some."

Jean grabs two bowls and two spoons from a small cabinet on the wall, places them on the table, and goes to the fireplace. He brings back the pot of stew, fills the bowls and takes it back.

"So, Thomas, I can tell you're running from somewhere. Just want to say that you're safe here." says Jean.

Thomas looks at Jean and says, "I know, and I appreciate your kindness," after a beat, he smiles and adds, "This stew is delicious."

As Jean and Thomas continue to eat, Jean looks over at Thomas and says, "You know, you can stay here as long as you need to. But I'm surprised at the fact that you haven't asked me for directions to head north. Usually that's the first thing runaways ask me when I meet them."

Thomas puts his spoon down, looks over at Jean and says, "Mr. Lavigne, I really do believe that God himself brought me to you. Yes, I was heading north originally, but my footsteps led me west, right to you. Now, for some reason I feel compelled to stay with you for a while."

"So, you're saying God brought you here?" asks Jean.

Thomas looks at Jean right in the eyes and says, "Jesus himself wants me to be sitting here talking to you right now."

Jean is surprised by what Thomas just said, and replies, "Well, tomorrow you can help me check on the traps on the southern part of the swamp. I will show you how to trap, and you can tell me more about this Jesus."

Thomas smiles wide and says, "I sure will."

The next morning Jean and Thomas are on a small boat, slowly moving through the water. Jean is slowly rowing the boat, and carefully watches as Thomas prepares one of the traps.

"That's right. Just like I showed you," says Jean.

"So, like I was sayin', it was a preacher man that came to the master's house and actually got permission to talk to us. He convinced master by telling him that we would be more obedient if we was Christians, you know," Thomas explains.

"Was he a priest?" asks Jean.

Thomas pauses for a moment, then replies, "A priest? I don't know what that is, but I do know he taught us the Bible. Reverend Bartholomew Johnson. I'll never forget his name. He read the Bible to us, and taught us to pray, to talk to God, just like I'm talking to you now."

The boat hits the shore, and Jean climbs out to check on one of the traps by the trees.

Thomas continues to speak, "The reverend, he visited us from week to week. He read to us from the good book and convinced a lot of us to accept Jesus Christ into our hearts."

"Did you do it? Accept Jesus?" asks Jean as he removes a dead gopher out of the hidden trap.

"I did! I sure did! It was the best thing that ever happened to me!" says Thomas.

"But you're still a slave, so what good did it do you?" asks Jean.

Thomas looks at Jean and beams. "God freed my mind. He freed my heart and my soul. This world don't matter. This just a testing ground to see who is gonna spend eternity where… You believe in Jesus and do the good, you goin' up to Heaven. You don't believe, you end up in Hell. And I'm not going to Hell! This life has been a hell for me already!" says Thomas.

Jean gets back into the boat. he puts the dead animal under a blanket, sits down and says, "I can understand that."

Thomas looks at Jean for a few minutes as Jean grabs the oars and begins to row the boat into a deeper part of the swamp. Jean looks around at the trees, to his left, and then to his right. He then looks at Thomas who is staring at him.

"What's the matter?" asks Jean.

"I know why I's here," says Thomas.

"Oh yeah?" Jean replies.

Thomas looks at Jean with a faraway look, almost as if he's looking past him. "God wants you to know that He has something for you to do. It's important, and only you can do it right."

Jean partly smiles and says, "So, God talks to you now?"

"I just got a knowing in my heart, that's all. That's why I'm here, to tell you about the Lord, so that you can do good. So you can get to Heaven."

Jean looks at Thomas as he continues to row toward his cabin, now visible in the distance. He wonders about the things that Thomas is saying, and says, "Thomas, I don't know if God sent you or not, but I can tell you're a good man."

Thomas puts the trap down, and says, "I was taking care of master's horses one evening, and it was raining outside. I had just finished breaking up the bale of hay and was about to go back to the house to see if master needed anything from me before I went to bed. I walked out of the barn, closed the door and looked at the big house, filled with lights. I heard the music and the laughing coming from inside; the master had some guests over. I wondered then if this is what my whole life would be like, me outside in the rain, with nothing but the clothes on my back. Suddenly, the dark sky fills with light, and lightning struck in the open field in front of the house.

"I ran out to see what the lightning had done to the ground, out of curiosity. There was a large black circle in the ground, and smoke came from it. I had never seen anything like it in my life. I was really scared. Then it happened again, further down the property. What are the

chances of that, I thought. I ran to it. I knew in my heart
that this meant something, so I just had to see. The rain
started to come down even harder. It was like a curtain.
When I finally got there, the dark mark on the ground
looked like an arrow pointing to the woods.

"I looked back toward the house, and I could not
see it, then I looked in the direction of the arrow, and there
was a clear path into the woods. So, I ran, in the rain, for a
whole three days. After that I walked and walked, for at
least another three days, the whole time feeling like I was
heading in the right direction. Finally got to this swamp
here, then you found me. I wouldn't call me good. I'm just
tryin' a survive."

The boat hits the shoreline next to Jean's cabin. Jean
stands up and gets out of the boat, and Thomas begins to
hand him supplies. Jean looks at Thomas as he hands him
empty traps, and dead animals, and then change of heart
takes hold of Jean. He decides at that point and time that he
is going to help Thomas escape. He could not stand to just
wait and do nothing anymore.

As the two carry the open traps and dead animals over to the cabin, Jean says, "Thomas, I know that there will be people looking for you. It is not safe for you to stay here. Tomorrow morning, you're going to take the extra boat and head north. I have a friend that lives at the edge of the swamp. His name is Benny. I'll write you a letter to give him, and he will help you. But you need to move on."

Thomas nods in approval, and says, "Alright…"

Jean smiles and says, "Can you tell me more about God?"

"I sure can," says Thomas.

The next morning, Jean is filling the boat with provisions at the bank of the swamp. It's early, the sun is just beginning to show its light through the trees, and there seems to be thousands of birds singing. The morning dew hangs heavy in the air still. The air is thick, and it's already getting hot. Jean looks over all the supplies on the boat, and everything seems to be in order.

Jean stands and smiles, proud of himself for helping Thomas. But then, out of nowhere, Jean hears yelling coming from the front side of his cabin. He runs to see what the commotion is all about. As he turns the corner of the cabin Jean sees five white men beating Thomas at the front of his house.

"Hey! Hey what are you doing?" yells Jean as he begins to approach the group, ready to fight.

Suddenly his front door opens and a sixth man walks out of his cabin. He quickly walks up to Jean and stops him. The man reaches into his pocket and pulls out a folded stack of bills. He holds it out to Jean, but Jean does not reach for it. He is transfixed on Thomas who is being badly beaten.

Jean looks at the man in front of him and says, "That's enough!"

"I'll say when enough is enough Jean," says the man as he brandishes a large butcher knife.

The man reaches for John's hands and puts the money in it then turns around to look at the beating. The men viciously beat Thomas. One of them knocks his teeth out with the butt of his rifle. Thomas slowly turns around on his belly and spits out more teeth as the men continue to beat him. Jean is frozen in fear and cannot move. He watches as Thomas looks up to the sky and screams.

"Jesus. Jesus!"

The men continue to beat him, and mock him until finally they slowly back away, realizing that Thomas was no longer moving. The man that gave Jean the money walks up to Thomas, and turns him over, revealing Thomas's bloody face. But to their surprise, it has a pleasant look on it. He is almost smiling.

Jean is in shock. Everything is happening so fast. He looks at the scene unfolding before him almost as if it is an out-of-body experience. Two of the men grab Thomas and throw his body into their boat. The men seem disappointed, and slowly board their boats.

One of them yells out to Jean, "Thanks for holding him for us Jean. We knew we could count on you… Be seeing you."

And just like that, the men are gone. Jean looks on as the boats drift away from him. As he stands there, distraught but steady, the money falls out of his hand. He looks down at the pool of blood on the ground where Thomas's body had been, and his teeth are still there.

"He died with a smile on his face," whispers Jean to himself.

Jean walks up to the puddle of blood and picks up Thomas's teeth. He looks at them and then looks up in the direction the boats left.

Jean goes into his cabin and sits at the table. He looks at a bag on his bed. It was supposed to be Thomas's change of clothes. Then he looks at the chair on the other side of the table, and in his mind, he can see Thomas talking to him about God. Jean puts the teeth on the table in front of him, and stares at them. Thomas's words come back to him, as though he is speaking.

"You got to give your heart to Jesus. It's not about this world, it's about what comes next."

The morning turns to night, and all Jean can do is just stare at the teeth as Thomas's words fill his mind. He had said so many things, so many encouraging things. Jean had not realized what a blessing Thomas had been, not until that moment. Heaviness engulfs Jean's heart, and he begins to weep—slowly at first, but little by little, the weeps turn into screams. Jean runs out of his cabin and into the night. He runs into the swamp and continues to run as he screams in pain until he gets to a small dirt island surrounded by green water.

Jean falls to his knees and looks up past the tree canopy and to the dark sky covered in stars.

"God!" yells Jean. "He was good to me, and I let him die!" Jean puts his head down to the ground and says, "Jesus, help me! I am horrible, I am terrible. He was my friend, and I let them kill him! Why? *Why?* He did not deserve that!"

Jean rips his shirt off in despair and continues to scream, "I'm sorry. I'm sorry! Please forgive me! Please forgive me! I want to do good! I want to do good like Thomas taught me!"

Jean puts his hands to his face as he continues to scream. The screams slowly turn back to sobbing, and then to complete silence. After a while, Jean stands. He wipes the tears from his face and says, "I'm gonna do good… I promise."

The words echo in Jean's memory as he tells this story to Isi, who is captivated by what he just told her. Jean comes out of the vivid flashback and sees Isi by his side looking at him.

Biisan, still at the fire, stirring the pot, looks back and says, "It's almost ready."

Jean looks at Isi and says, "I swore to God on that day that I would spend the rest of my life helping people. So, with His help, I try to show kindness to others… And you?"

"Well…" says Isi.

There is a quiet pause as Isi and Jean look into the camp. They see natives sitting by their fires, some sleeping, some eating. A soldier passes by and pushes a native man out of his way, and the man falls. The soldier looks at the man lying on the ground, waiting for him to do something, or say something, but the man just looks away. The soldier spits and walks into the darkness.

Isi looks up at the sky and says, "It was not long ago that my people ruled these lands. We had freedom, love and family. We tried to get along with neighboring tribes. Sometimes we fought, sometimes we had peace, but we respected one another. We kept our word to each other.

"Then the white man came, smiling as a friend, offering help, and taking land. And we did help. We did teach you how to live on this land and shared with you many of our secrets.

"But that was not enough. Your ways are most devious, because in the name of safety and your God, you coerced us into surrendering our land. You whites…killed our people, our families and our children and took more land.

"Your thirst for what we had could not be quenched. Because no matter how much we gave, no matter how much land we surrendered to you, you took more and more. You continued as if you had the right to rape our women, to kill our children, and desecrate our holy places.

"And today we are being altogether moved from our ancestral land, taken away from all that we know… In the name of safety, and in the name of your God…

"I feel sadness—sadness so deep, and so wide, an ocean could fit in it. I feel a burning anger, an unstoppable rage for what has happened to my people and cannot relate to your experience with your God.

"I know what I have seen. I know what has happened to my people, and what is happening now. And to be fair, I also know that during all this madness and death, you have been kind to me, you have been merciful, you…have been a friend.

"That, I understand." Isi stretches out her hand to Jean.

He sees it, takes it and holds it. Jean looks at Isi with sadness in his eyes and says, "I'm sorry… For…everything."

"Me too," says Isi as she wipes a tear from her eyes. Isi stands and walks up to Biisan who is still stirring the pot. She leans forward, takes in the aroma coming out of the stew and smiles. She looks at Biisan and nods in approval, he smiles back. She turns back to Jean. "I know why I'm here, on this trail, but why are you men making this journey?"

Jean stands, walks up to Isi, stands beside her and says, "My business has taken me to many places. Cities, towns, and I've crossed a lot of open land. But to me, there's nothing more beautiful than the Northwest Territories. Beautiful mountains, green fields, and forests as far as the eye can see. Lakes, rivers and plenty of game.

"I built a large cabin next to a lake a few years back. It's surrounded by thousands of acres of open land. There's a small town east of my cabin, and I'm setting up a trading post there. That's where we're going."

Isi wipes a tear from her eye, forces a smile and says, "That sounds nice…"

Jean turns to Isi and says, "You can come live with us there Isi. You and your sister. You're more than welcome to come."

Isi puts her head down when Jean mentions her sister. The pain of her going missing stabs her in the heart. She is so worried for her and not knowing where she is pains her.

Jean sees Isi's reaction and says, "We will find her, I promise. As soon as these soldiers leave, I will mount up a search for her."

Isi nods without saying a word.

Chapter 9: The Hunters

It's a cold but bright afternoon. Large cumulous clouds above move quickly through the sky, allowing the bright rays of the sun to shine down on the river below. Birds chirp in the trees, as they sway from side to side due to the cold bursts of wind passing by. The birds fly from one side of the river to the other, past Abeke, who is close to the riverbank, knee deep with spear in hand, looking at the fish a few feet away. She looks up at the sky and sees the weather is changing quickly. Dark clouds are beginning to take over the sky and a light, powdery snow begins to fall.

In the stillness of the moment, Abeke feels, then sees her water break. It falls into the river below. She grabs her stomach with one hand and uses the spear as a walking stick as she makes her way to land. Abeke gets a sharp pain and drops the spear in the water to hold her belly as she leans forward.

"Rebecca! Tula!" yells Abeke. Carefully, Abeke takes a step toward the shore, making sure her footing is secure. "Tula! Rebecca! I need your help, girls!" yells Abeke again.

She takes another step, and when she looks up, she is surprised to sees Abit, Captain Francis's tracker, standing right in front of her.

"Who are you?" Abeke asks, but she is suddenly met by his fist to her face. She falls backward into the water.

Abit looks back toward the campfire the girls had made, and there is Captain Francis holding Rebecca. He throws her down to the ground, and quickly gets on top of her. He has one hand over her mouth, keeping her from screaming, as he holds her down with his other hand.

"Well look at you… Aren't you a pretty thing?" asks the captain.

Then as he slowly moves his hand from her mouth, he tells her, "I don't mean you any harm. You're not who we're looking for. Just answer a few questions for me."

"Let me go!" says Rebecca.

She bites the captain's hand so hard that she draws blood. He retracts and holds his hand in pain. He leans up and shifts his weight, and Rebecca squirms out from underneath him. She frantically pushes herself away from him, grabs a large stick and tries to stand, but the captain reaches out and pushes her down again.

He looks down at the bleeding bite mark on his hand and says, "Now you just pissed me off."

Rebecca tries to push herself up off the ground, the captain sees her and kicks her down a gain. She hits her jaw on a rock, splitting her bottom lip. Rebecca lifts her bloody face and begins to crawl on her belly as she tries to get away.

"You look like a worm crawling through the dirt," the captain laughs as he kicks her on the stump of her missing leg.

Rebecca cries out in pain. She continues to crawl, trying to get away from the captain, but he is having too much fun. He follows her as she slowly pushes herself through the brush and dirt. He kicks her again, and again.

"Leave me alone!" she cries out.

But the captain smiles. He reaches down and picks Rebecca up with one hand, turns her around and brings her face right up to his as he holds her suspended in midair.

"Where's the little Indian girl?"

Rebecca does not answer but looks at the captain with defiance.

The captain slaps Rebecca across the face with an open palm, splitting her bottom lip even more. "Tell Me!" yells the captain.

But she is done being a pawn to a man. She looks at him and spits blood in his face.

The captain smiles, as he holds Rebecca up with one hand and wipes some of the blood off his face with the other hand and licks it.

"It didn't have to be this way. I just wanted the slave and the Indian. I would have brought you back to civilization. Pretty white girl like you coulda still had some type of life, even with a leg missing." The captain closes his hand and makes a fist. He pulls it back, smiles, and punches Rebecca in the eye, leaving her stunned.

"Now, I'm gonna beat you bloody," says the captain as he punches her again. Then he headbutts her, splitting the edge of her brow open, blood splattering everywhere. "Then, when I find the Indian, I'm gonna come back and fuck you bloody." He repeatedly punches her, bringing her face in with one hand as he punches her with the other. "Then I'll hang you from a tree and let the forest critters have the rest of you," says the captain as he continues to beat Rebecca's face with his fist. "Where is the native bitch?" the captain screams in the woman's face.

Rebecca looks at the captain through her swollen eyes, her face covered in blood. She tries to say something but can hardly form the words.

The captain brings her face right up against his and says, more gently, "Where is she? Where is that Indian girl?"

Rebecca looks at the captain as tears fall from her eyes onto her bloody face. She tries to breathe as blood comes out of her mouth, tries to say something, but can't, as her jaw seems to be locked up.

"Just look in the direction she went. That's all I need; I know she's not far."

Rebecca looks into the woods to the left of the captain.

The captain bears an evil grin, licks a tear from her bloody face and says, "That wasn't so hard now, was it?"

He headbutts Rebecca and slams her body like a rag doll against one of the nearby trees. She falls to the ground unconscious. The captain grabs a rock close to the campfire, kneels in front of Rebecca and smashes her face with it.

But he doesn't stop there. He continues, the grotesque sound of the rock colliding with her face echoing into the surrounding wilderness.

The captain smashes her face with the stone so hard that her face completely caves in. The captain looks down at the bloody mess, shakes his head and then quickly makes his way into the woods.

The trees and brush are thick. Everything is now covered in a light powdery snow. After just a few minutes, he comes across a small clearing. The captain crouches down and observes from behind a bush. He knows he found her. He sees firewood piled up in the middle, with a bow and arrows, and a small bag with provisions. He waits for a few minutes, then he finally sees her. Tula comes out of the opposite side of the clearing with an armful of firewood. She drops it onto the large pile she has been gathering.

Captain Francis slowly comes out from behind cover and enters the clearing. "So you're the slippery rabbit…" he says.

Tula jumps back, surprised by the monstrous man before her. She looks over at her bow and arrow, then runs toward them, but the captain quickly jumps in her way, and backhands Tula, knocking her backward.

"Oh no, little rabbit. We'll have none of that!" says the captain.

Tula, stunned, climbs to her feet, but before she does, the captain slaps her again, hard. Tula falls to the ground again. The captain reaches down and grabs Tula by the neck and picks her up. The little girl punches and kicks into the air.

"Let me go! What are you doing?" Tula says in Choctaw.

The captain laughs and says, "You need to learn to speak English. I don't know what you're saying!"

Not too far away, by the riverbank, Abeke sits up, still shaken from the hit she received. She looks up and sees Abit standing over her. Abeke quickly turns on her hands and knees and tries to get into the river, but Abit grabs her by her shirt, and begins to drag her back to shore. Abeke turns to face Abit and kicks him repeatedly as she tries to get away. Abit reaches down, grabs Abeke, and puts her in a bear hug, face to face. He walks her back to shore. He walks her closer to camp, and when she sees Rebecca bloody on the ground, Abeke headbutts Abit.

He lets her go, stumbles backward, and puts his hand up to his bleeding nose.

Abeke runs toward Rebecca and turns her around and shakes her.

"Rebecca! Rebecca, get up!" Abeke says, as she sees Abit moving toward her.

Abit opens his side pouch and takes out a pair of iron shackles.

Abeke sees them and says, "No way… No way!"

Abit lunges at Abeke and tries to grab her right wrist. She punches his shoulder repeatedly. He trips, and they fall in the struggle. Abit reaches to grab her left wrist, but Abeke pulls away and punches his bloody nose. Abit grabs his nose in pain, and she takes the opportunity to get up. As she does, though, a sharp pain rushes from her midsection and she grabs her belly. Abit reaches out to grab Abeke's right arm, and as he is about to shackle her, she kicks him in the groin.

"I said *no!*" screams Abeke.

As Abit falls to his knees, Abeke quickly looks around the area for a weapon, and her eyes widen as she looks over at the riverside. She makes a run for the water, entering it as she falls to her knees to reach into the water.

"Ahh," she says, fighting off the pain of another contraction. "Baby, you're just gonna have to wait a little longer…" says Abeke as she cradles her belly with her free hand.

Abit stands up, enraged now. He wipes the blood from his face, but it continues to flow like a river from his broken nose, down to his chest. He looks around and sees Abeke in the water. Her back is toward him. Abit pulls out his hunting knife and runs toward Abeke. Abeke turns to look at Abit as he runs toward her, but she does not move.

Abit lets fly a war cry as he runs to a large boulder and jumps off it, and lunging toward Abeke.

Abeke waits until Abit is in midair, and quickly raises her spear, anchoring it in the sediment below. Abit cannot change his momentum, and falls right into it. The spear pierces his ribcage and exits through the back of his right shoulder. For a moment, Abit is suspended in the air by the spear itself, until Abeke lets go of it, and he splashes into the water. Abeke stands up, and looks at Abit as he twitches, gargles and urinates into the water. She reaches down and grabs the knife out of his hand.

"I'm never going in shackles again… *Never*!"

Abit is slowly taken away by the current, spear and all.

Abeke slowly makes her way to the shore. She puts one foot out of the water, and a sharp labor pain hit her, bringing her to her knees. She hears a scream in the distance and looks in that direction.

"Tula…"

A short distance away, Captain Francis has overpowered Tula and is now on top of her. Tula screams again as the captain rips pieces of her clothing off, leaving the young girl exposed. Tula struggles to get away, but the captain holds her hands and neck with one hand, as he rips another piece of her clothing off.

"You're gonna learn little rabbit…" says the captain.

"Leave me alone. Help! *Help*!" screams Tula

The captain reaches down to sniff her, and Tula wriggles a hand free and scratches his left eye, drawing blood from his brow.

The captain becomes enraged. "I'm gonna split you in half you little bitch!"

As he secures Tula with his left arm, shifting all his weight on top of her, he takes down his trousers with his other hand.

"No! Help! Abeke! Rebecca!" screams Tula

The captain spits on his free hand, and as he reaches down to his groin, he suddenly stops, and his eyes widen. He looks behind him and sees an arrow stuck to his shoulder.

"What the fu—?"

Another arrow thuds into his shoulder, just a few inches away from the first. The captain reaches to get one of the arrows, and another arrow wizzes by his head, barely missing him. The arrow embeds into a tree a few feet away.

The captain stands. His pants completely fall on the ground, revealing his nakedness. Abeke stands across from him, just a few yards away. She bends her bow again and releases another arrow. The arrow meets its mark in his upper left thigh. The captain reaches for it as he screams.

"Ahh! What the fuck? I'm gonna kill you!"

The captain pulls the arrow out of his thigh, reaches back and pulls the other two arrows out of his back. Abeke looks around, but she is completely out of arrows. The captain shambles toward her as fast as he can, and just as he is about to reach Abeke, a mountain lion jumps out of the woods, and onto the captain's back, sinking its teeth deep into his neck.

Blood sprays out from the wound, painting the tree leaves above crimson. The captain falls to his knees as he reaches back to grab the lion, but he can't reach it. The lion takes another bite, this time piercing a major artery, blood pours onto his chest and the ground below. The captain falls to the ground, reaching impotently for the lion on his back, struggling until the lion jumps off him. The captain, on his back, struggles to move away, but the lion readies himself for another strike, it's face covered in the captain's blood.

"Give me my rifle…or it will kill us all!" gasps the captain to the girls as he extends his hand to them.

The captain slowly pushes himself to his knees and when he does, an arrow lands on his chest. Surprised, he looks over at the girls and sees Tula now holding the bow.

"You're the only one he's after," says Tula.

The lion jumps on the captain's chest, biting him right in the face. The captain falls backward, hardly resisting anymore.

An unsettling crack resounds as the lion breaks the captain's jaw. The girls jump back and watch as the lion pulls the twitching body of the captain away from them, leaving a trail of blood behind. The lion leaves the body of the captain for a moment and slowly walks up to the girls and sits upright in front of them. The girls are still, not knowing what will happen next. Slowly and deliberately, the lion looks over at Tula, looks back at the captain's body, then looks back at her, right into her eyes. A few moments later, the lion gets up, goes to the captain, and continues to drag him into the woods.

Abeke and Tula slowly step backward as they watch the captain's body disappear behind the heavy brush. Tula looks at Abeke and sees a small trail of blood coming down her leg.

"Abeke! Abeke, are you hurt?" asks Tula.

Abeke looks down at herself, grabs her belly and says, "The baby's coming!"

"Where is Rebecca?" asks Abeke, as she holds onto Tula. "I don't know!" responds Tula as she helps Abeke back to their camp.

The girls make their way through the forest, enter their camp and slowly walk toward one of the large trees by the river.

"Here, sit right here. I'm getting some cloths and the bucket for water," says Tula.

"They should be close to the campfire. Rebecca was right there, did she leave?" asks Abeke, then she screams in pain. "Ahh! Hurry. Hurry Tula!"

Tula runs to the campfire and there she sees Rebecca by a tree, covered under a light layer of snow. She's dead, the snow turning red as it lands on her. Even that doesn't hide her grisly fate. Her face has been completely bashed in by the blows that the captain gave her earlier. Tula turns away and throws up. She begins to cry, but throws up again.

"Tula! Hurry!" Abeke yells out.

Tula wipes her face with her forearm, grabs the bucket, and a few pieces of clothing from one of the bags. She runs back to Abeke in tears. She places the shirts besides Abeke and runs to the river.

"Ahh!" yells Abeke, she looks down, and the head of the baby is already visible.

Tula runs back with a bucket full of water, crying.

"What's the matter?" asks Abeke. "I'm the one in pain. Why are you crying?"

Tula places the bucket down, grabs a shirt, and soaks it in the water. She looks at Abeke in the eyes and says, "I found Rebecca…"

"No!" cries Abeke.

Tula nods as she continues to sob.

Abeke screams once more, emotional turmoil mixing with the tremendous pain of the ongoing labor.

Chapter 10: The Final Push

The light of the rising sun can be seen in the distance beyond the hills. Birds chirp in the trees as they welcome the morning, flying from tree to tree. A cold wind moves through the branches. The mild days of autumn are fading away, and the coldness of winter slowly begins to creep in, taking hold of the land, one day at a time. Below the tree canopy, Tula, Abeke and the newborn baby are sleeping together, holding each other for warmth under a few blankets beside a small campfire. A thin layer of frost covers the ground all around them.

The telltale sound of footfalls crunching through the thin layer of snow can be heard drawing closer to them.

Abeke slowly opens her eyes. She is suddenly startled by what she sees, but the shock quickly turns to relief as she recognizes the friendly face. "Talako! What are you doing here? You scared me!" says Abeke, her words rousing Tula from her sleep as well.

Talako stands over the girls with a wide smile on his face and his hands behind his back.

"Talako!" says Tula as she gets up and hugs the old man.

Talako begins to laugh and pats Tula on the back as she hugs him. "I am glad to see you are well. We were all worried for you," he says.

Tula pulls away from Talako and excitedly says, "Two men attacked us a few days ago! They killed our friend, and they almost had us!"

"One of them was a native, he was gonna put me in chains again!" says Abeke, enthusiastically shaking her head as she sits up. She picks up her baby and brings him to her bosom.

"I know, I know. That's why I am here," says Talako as he squats to be at Abeke's eye level. "I had no rest after you girls left my camp. I worried so much that my sleep left me. I knew I should have tried to convince you to stay with us. It was not long after you left that two strange men came looking for you. I found that very suspicious. We knew you were in trouble, so a few warriors and I set out to find you, to make sure you were well," says Talako.

"They're dead," says Tula.

Out from behind the trees, twelve native warriors come out of hiding and reveal themselves. Talako stands and says, "We know. We found their remains on our way here. One of them looked like—"

"A mountain lion attacked him!" says Abeke.

"Like a mountain lion ate him," Talako finishes. "There was very little left of that man. We also found a fresh grave…." says Talako.

"Rebecca," Tula says, bowing her head in respect. "She was our friend."

"One of them killed her," Abeke says.

"So, will you travel with us now?" asks Talako.

The girls look at each other, then at Talako.

"Yes!" The girls say at the same time.

Talako smiles and nods his head in approval. Talako looks at Abeke's baby, and she hands the boy to him. He carefully takes the child and holds it close to his chest, caressing his forehead.

*   *   *

Meanwhile, many miles away, Jean and Isi ride on the front of the wagon, amid thousands of people, fighting against nature. The trail seems endless. A snowfall from the previous night has covered the land, making the wagons move slowly, and the people traveling with them even slower. The weather has completely changed. It is bitter cold, and windy. The many weeks of travel have really worn the people down.

Everyone moves at a slower pace. The gray clouds above that cover the sky constantly, and the cold wind that now hits them head on do little to help the mood of the people. Morale could not be any lower as famine, pestilence and death spread without containment. Depression grips the populace, and lack of a will to live takes deep root into the travelers' hearts.

The horses of Jean's wagon suddenly move to the left, and Isi looks down and sees they are avoiding a dead corpse, a native woman face down in the mud and snow. Isi looks on as the wagon passes her and continues to move.

"They're not burying their dead?" asks Isi.

Jean looks at her solemnly and says, "Maybe she was the last one in her family… Or maybe they could not carry her, I don't know."

"Maybe we should—" Isi begins to say.

"Go back, pick her up and bury her later? I don't think we should right now. That's not the first person I've seen abandoned like that. Neither have you," says Jean.

"I know," says Isi.

Biisan, who was sitting in the back of the wagon, moves up to the front to take a look and says, "I've never seen such misery. We are people, people who had dreams, desires and families. At one point in their lives, they wanted something more. They don't deserve this. We don't deserve this.

"No one deserves such cruelty," he goes on. "We don't know what diseases are killing these folks, like that lady. Whatever it is it's traveling fast amongst the people. It's dangerous. We should stay away from dead bodies like that."

A burst of cold wind hits them all of a sudden. They grab onto their jackets and try to shield themselves with their coats.

"The weather has definitely changed… So cold," says Isi, but no one responds.

They all listen as the sounds of the caravan echo through the trees—the rattle of the wagons and the horses, soldiers on horseback barking out orders to keep everyone moving. The people moaning and coughing, children crying and the steps of hundreds of hungry, homeless, displaced people making their way to an unknown land resonates throughout the wilderness.

A middle-aged native man slowly makes his way to Jean's wagon on horseback from the left. Jean catches a glimpse of him as he approaches through his peripheral vision. He turns to him and nods, but the man does not respond and continues to approach. Jean keeps an eye on him until the native man rides his horse right beside him. The man looks at Jean for a minute without saying a word. It begins to snow.

"How can I help you friend?" says Jean.

"Are you called Jean?" asks the man.

"Yes, my name is Jean. What can I do for you?"

The man takes a necklace from his front pocket and holds it out to Jean. Jean reaches and slowly takes the necklace, wondering what all this is about.

"I am Chochmo… Atepa's brother. A while ago you helped her when she was in need, and for that I am grateful. She said you showed her kindness. You fed her and her young boy."

Jean holds out the necklace and sees that it's a beautiful piece of native craftsmanship, he quickly looks at the man and asks, "How is she doing? How's her child?" asks Jean.

Chochmo looks at Jean with faraway eyes, takes a deep breath and says, "She's dead, along with the child."

Jean's mouth drops, and he is immediately stricken by the news.

Isi who is sitting beside him leans over to look at Chochmo and asks, "How? How did this happen? What happened to them?"

Chochmo's eyes become glazed over and he struggles to speak, but eventually finds the words.

"A few weeks ago, her boy fell down with a fever. The boy started coughing. Sometimes for hours on end. We tried many remedies and treatments, but nothing seemed to work. She carried the boy bundled up to her chest during the day and kept him close beside her during the night. The boy did not wake up one morning, and Atepa was devastated. She refused to believe her boy was no longer there, and continued to carry his body, wrapped to her chest during the day, and kept him the same way during the night. We urged her to let the boy go. We told her that his spirit was no longer there, the boy had moved on, but she refused to let the body go. She said she wanted to give him a proper burial—a native burial—when we got to the new land. This went on for many days. Atepa stopped eating, she stopped sleeping. She stayed up all night humming songs to her boy. Yesterday morning, when we were on the trail, she fell, and did not get up. Almost as if that's what she had wanted all along, I think. To go and be with her child."

Speechless, Isi and Jean look at Chochmo with dismay, devastated by the horrible news.

"I'm so sorry Chochmo," says Jean, and then he holds up the necklace. "So, this necklace was hers? Here, take it back. I can't take this."

"It was. And you should have it. You helped them when nobody else would," says Chochmo.

Jean takes a good look at the necklace. It is very intricate and carved with beautiful detail. He turns to Chochmo and says, "Are you going to be okay? Do you need anything?"

Chochmo looks around to the people walking through the snow, and the wagons ahead of him. He glances at Jean and says, "Allow me to travel beside your wagon for a while…"

Jean smiles and says, "Of course. You can stay as long as you like. It would be our pleasure to have you join us. We would love the company!"

Chochmo nods in approval. Without saying a word, he continues to ride besides Jean's wagon in silence. The powdery snow slowly turns into thick and heavy snow, the wind gusts turn into a steady blow of arctic air resisting every movement they make. The day is long, and when evening comes, more than three feet of snow have accumulated where they will spend the night. They clear large areas to set up encampments and build fires, but it still not enough to get warm.

The next morning Jean hears a knocking on the back of his wagon.

"Mr. Lavigne! Mr. Lavigne! I need to have a word with you please!" says Major O'Connell.

There is no response, so the major knocks again.

"Mr. Lavigne I am standing in the snow, in the freezing cold, the sun has not yet come up. I will not be long, I just need to have a word with you, sir!" says the major, now a bit frustrated.

The back tarp of the wagon opens. Jean, Biisan and Isi stare at the major from underneath what seems a mountain of blankets. Jean looks at the overcast sky.

"Another gloomy day…" Jean says.

"Mr. Lavigne," says the major.

"Yes, yes Major, what can I do for you on this horrific morning?" asks Jean.

The major is a bit taken aback by the comment, but proceeds to say, "Well, we will be coming to the journey's end here in a few days. You may or may not know, but we have already entered the new Indian territory."

"I am aware," replies Jean.

"My company will act as an escort for the next two days, and at that point and time, when the Indians are deep into their new land, we will depart and winter southeast of their territory. I wanted to see if you would join us. If so, you would be traveling and staying with me and my lieutenants," says the major.

"No," Jean quickly answers.

The major is surprised by his answer, and says, "Mr. Lavigne, I recognize you and I may not have always seen eye to eye, but we do need your help. A man of your experience and abilities to relate to these folks can be very valuable asset."

"I'm not interested, Major," says Jean.

"If its compensation you seek, I can definitely arrange that. You would be providing the U.S. Army a great service," says the major.

"How many people died during the night, Major?" asks Jean.

The major pauses for a few seconds, looks over at his guards, then turns to looks at Jean and says, "My men gave counted 23 bodies this morning. All perished during the night."

"How many children amongst them?" asks Jean.

"Six. Maybe seven if you count teenagers. But what does this have to do with what I'm asking?" asks the major, clearly frustrated by the questioning.

"Everything! It has everything to do with what you're asking. You have the power to help these people, yet you watch them die without batting an eye! You have all the help you need. These men, women and children have nothing! My place is not with you. Not anymore," says Jean.

"Mr. Lavigne!" says the major.

"Thank you Major, but it's a no," says Jean. He looks over to Biisan and Isi, then looks back at the major and says, "I will be staying with my family."

The major looks at Jean with complete disgust. His lips quiver as he is hardly able to keep himself still. "Fine! Have it your way! We don't need you!" screams the major as he throws out his hands in exasperation.

He takes a long look at Jean, Biisan and Isi, shakes his head and storms away from the wagon. His guards quickly follow behind him. As the men leave, the major slips, but is quickly caught by one of his men.

Jean looks up at the sky as it begins to snow again, then over to the white, snow-covered landscape filled with natives in tents, under blankets, some already walking around or prepping for the day, and packing up their belongings. He looks back at Isi and Biisan, takes a deep breath, and nods.

"So, I'm your family now?" asks Isi with a smile.

Biisan pushes her shoulder in jest and says, "I always wanted a sister!"

Jean smiles and says, "Yeah, after what we've been through, we are definitely family now."

Isi smiles and nods saying, "Good… This is good."

*   *   *

Two months later, in what is present-day Oklahoma, Tula and Abeke, with her baby on a cradleboard, reach the top of a snowy hill on horseback, and join a few native men already there. Everyone is bundled up in winter clothing. They look over a vast open land covered in snow, almost barren, with very little vegetation as far as the eye can see. A big gust of wind picks up the powdery snow, carrying it their way, and hits their faces like sand. They all shrug and shield themselves. The sun rays pierce the numerous moving clouds above, landing sporadically throughout the land as if they are dancing. Far in the distance, they spot what looks to be the beginnings of a settlement. Talako walks up to the girls and pats their horses as he passes them. He heads over to the edge of the hill to get a better look below.

In the settlement below the large hill, Isi is on top of a wagon, taking provisions from the tail of the wagon to the front. Biisan approaches the back of the wagon with a large box and places it on the back of the wagon for Isi to take. Jean has a list in his hand and is looking at a pile of provisions on the ground right beside them.

All around them, people are building homes, and wagons with supplies move past them. People are busy with their comings and goings. Framework for buildings are being erected. People are trying to build something permanent here. A small boy walking by Jean points towards a hill on the outskirts of the settlement—the hill where Tula and the others are.

"Look at the people on the mountain!" says the boy, and everyone looks up.

Isi looks at the child pointing, then to where he points. She stands as Jean approaches the wagon. He looks up at the hill, they look at each other, then they look back up at the hill.

"More of our people have arrived..." says Isi.

Up on the hill, more and more people arrive at the edge of the hill to get a look down at the settlement. People through the camp take note and stop working to looks at the people on the hill.

"Let's go and greet them," says Jean.

"I'll stay here with the wagon. You guys go on…" says Biisan.

Isi nods, and with Jean's help, she jumps off the wagon. They both walk to the edge of the settlement. Jean and Isi join a group of people looking on as the party slowly makes their way down the hill. Isi steps in front of the group to get a better look, and waves at the people coming.

Tula approaches the settlement on horseback with Abeke beside her, surrounded by Talako's people. As Tula looks at the people at the edge of the settlement, she sees a young woman waving her hand, and she recognizes her.

"Isi?" Tula whispers.

Tula snaps the reins of her horse and kicks with her heels. The horse bursts into a gallop, and Tula quickly passes everyone as she makes her way down the hill.

"Isi! Isi! It's me!" screams Tula as she rides.

Down at the edge of the settlement, Isi sees that a horse has broken away from the rest and is quickly coming toward them. Isi recognizes the way the rider is moving and says, "Tula?"

Tula, now close to the settlement's edge clearly sees Isi, who is now running towards her. Tula saps the reins of her horse again, tears flying in the wind as she smiles wide. The girls meet at the edge of the settlement yards away from everyone else. Tula jumps off her horse and runs towards Isi.

The girls clash in a powerful embrace of love, holding each other tightly. They cry in a euphoric moment, like a dream that has finally come true. The girls pull away slightly to look at each other.

"You've grown so much!" says Isi.

"I've missed you so much!" says Tula.

The girls embrace again as the group of people watching approach them, Jean included, as he stands a few feet away from the smiling girls. Abeke and the rest of Talako's people join the group. They all begin to greet each other, and the two groups become one.

A young, good-looking native teenage boy comes out of the crowd and calls out to Abeke, "Abeke! Abeke!" the boy yells.

Abeke immediately turns to look. She knows that voice. "Tashka?" says Abeke.

Tashka runs up to Abeke and they stand eye to eye.

"Yes, yes, it's me… Please believe me, I had no idea what my parents had planned until it was too late. I'm so sorry! I was sent into town the day they came for you, otherwise I would have stopped them! I was so angry with my parents for what they did to you!" says Tashka.

"Are they here?" asks Abeke.

"No. No, I left them. I'm here alone… But not anymore," replies Tashka as he reaches out to Abeke. She takes his hand, and he continues to say, "I left my parents and the farm. I've been looking for you for a long time now. From town to town, I looked, but no one seemed to know anything about your whereabouts. Or maybe they pretended not to know. After a few months, I ran into some soldiers who were rounding up the people. I was forced to join the migration…and here I am.”

Abeke and Tashka look at each other for a moment, remembering what they had. Abeke’s eyes begin to water.

Tashka says, “I still love you Abeke, please…”

Abeke leans forward and embraces Tashka. He lovingly hugs her back, and they hold one another for a few moments, then kiss. Abeke lightly pulls away. She takes the cradleboard from her back and shows Tashka their baby.

“I want you to meet your son,” says Abeke, and Tashka takes the baby and holds him close.

Tula walks Isi over to where Abeke is standing and says to Isi, “We have a new sister. Her name is Abeke. She saved me many times while we were on the trail.”

“We saved each other,” says Abeke.

Isi walks up to Abeke and tenderly hugs her, then caresses her face and says, "Thank you. Thank you for watching over her. Come, we have a lot to talk about!"

The settlers usher the travelers into their new settlement. It's a new land, a new chapter, a new beginning.

The End

Epilogue

It is a beautiful, bright sunny summer day with just a few clouds in the sky. At the edge of a lake stands a large wooden structure, a trading post, surrounded by very tall evergreen trees. Mountains in the distance, still covered in snow, round out the landscape. A dog barks as Isi, now pregnant with child, comes to the front door carrying a large sack of feed. She carries it through the porch, down the steps, and puts it in the back of a wagon, the large dog following her every step of the way.

"You didn't have to carry that. I could have done it for you," says an old white man sitting on the seat of the wagon.

"I'm more than capable but thank you Mr. Broder. We appreciate your business," says Isi with a smile as she wipes her brow.

"Of course, Isi. And tell your husband goodbye for me," says Mr. Broder. He tips his hat, snaps the reins to get his horses moving, and is on his way.

Isi watches as the wagon disappears through the trees, and into the forest as she pets her dog on the head. Jean comes out from behind the trading post with a wheelbarrow full of apples. He leaves it close to the trading post steps and walks over to Isi. Jean puts one arm around Isi and caresses her pregnant belly with the other. She kisses him on the lips and smiles.

"Hey Isi!" screams Abeke in the distance.

Isi and Jean look up and see Abeke, Tula, now a teenager, and a five-year-old riding a two-horse wagon that comes toward them. Isi and Jean wave at them as they approach. The wagon stops in front of them, Tula jumps off and runs to hug Isi.

"You should see it, guys. Tashka has a whole field full of potatoes now, and next week we'll start harvesting the pear trees!" says Tula.

"And how is Thomas? He is getting so big!" says Jean as Abeke's little boy jumps off the wagon, runs to him and hugs him.

"Hi Uncle Jean!" says the boy as Jean gives him a big hug.

Abeke ties the reins to the brake of the wagon and holds her hand out to Jean, who quickly takes her hand and helps her down. Abeke is heavily pregnant and makes her way down slowly.

"We are thankful for your help Tula, especially now," says Abeke.

"That's what family is for…" says Tula.